CATHERINE RYAN HYDE

WALTER'S PURPLE HEART

A NOVEL

Simon & Schuster

New York   London   Toronto   Sydney   Singapore

SIMON & SCHUSTER
Rockefeller Center
1230 Avenue of the Americas
New York, NY 10020

For information regarding special discounts for bulk purchases,
please contact Simon & Schuster Special Sales at 1-800-456-6798
or business@simonandschuster.com

Designed by Jeanette Olender
Manufactured in the United States of America

1   3   5   7   9   10   8   6   4   2

Library of Congress Cataloging-in-Publication Data is available.

ISBN 0-684-86723-0

For every life cut short by war

Walter's Purple Heart

CHAPTER ONE

Walter

Usually when the hero dies the story is over. Until I get half my head blown off, this story can't even begin.

Don't think I have a big ego, just because I call myself a hero. Anybody can be a hero after they're dead, even me. So, you see, there's an upside to being found dead at the opening credits. There's also a price tag.

But anyway, I'm holding up the story. I should hurry up and die.

Before I do, I need to stress a point. None of this was my idea. I was minding my own business from the word go.

This first small part I'll blame on the radio. After that it all falls squarely into Andrew's court. Andrew masterminded the whole disaster. I'm the kind of guy goes along for the ride. People say I should break that pattern, and maybe they're right, only I won't live long enough to try.

Here's where a good life fell down.

It's the coldest part of the year, December, with a wind like dry ice across the boardwalk, and Andrew and me, we're leaning on my dad's Ford. Nobody out but us and the seagulls, because honestly, who else would be so much the fool?

Andrew spins the dial on the car radio, settles on a station playing "String of Pearls." Cranks it up full blast. Me, I'm busy trying to get my damn Lucky lit against that high, cold wind, working with these fingers I can't even feel.

Then the music stops, and then the man comes on the radio and tells it.

Then I'm as good as dead.

Now most folks, they wouldn't blame that part on the radio. They'd likely blame it on the Japs.

Me, I like to put things in a real perspective. Tragic stuff happens every day, all over the world, but if you don't tell me, I won't know. Andrew won't know. Then Andrew won't need to run off half-cocked, and I won't have to go along for the ride.

Some people say I don't have to do anything unless I want to, but they're them. They don't know what it is to be me.

I'm holding up the story again. I should get on with the dying.

I could tell you where I am and how I got here, but I'd only be wasting your time. The real people, the live ones, the ones who own this story once I'm gone, they'll get to that soon enough. And get to it, and get to it. Live people get real into wheres and hows and whats. It's like a hobby with them.

Did I mention that this all happened decades ago? Sometimes I forget to mention the most basic things.

And I know when I talk about it, it doesn't sound decades old. I know I talk about it like I'm in it, right now. Like it's happening. And there's a reason for that. But it's hard to explain to anybody who isn't dead. Think of it like this: You know how there's time, and you have to be in one certain place in it? Well, that's you. That's not me.

Anyway, that radio thing, that was the beginning of a good life falling down. Now I'll tell you how it ends.

This is where I am.

I'm wading in a swamp in a jungle. Andrew's there, plus about ten other guys from my outfit. One goes ahead, one behind, to watch for crocodiles. If they see one, they shoot it. We also got scorpions, wasps, some giant mosquitoes, but nobody to protect us from them. Every man for himself.

The swamp stinks. The whole goddamned island stinks, like something used to be alive under there, only not recently.

We stumble up onto dry land.

We got our rifles slung over our shoulders now, nice and easy, and I'm lighting up a smoke. Because, see, we just heard that the Tokyo Night Express came and stole the last of our Japs.

We're on a cakewalk.

We're headed back to Henderson Field, relieved of the

worst duty known to man, flushing well-armed Japs out of caves on Mt. Austen. You never really know how awful a job is until that magic moment when you get to stop.

Morale is way up.

We walk in clusters, talking, laughing; somebody chews on me about something, but I'm too happy to listen or care.

It's the first time I've been happy since I got out of the hospital, no, since Hutch lobbed the mortar round that put me there. No, since I took the action that put me dead center on that round. But I forgot. I don't talk about that. Most things I'll tell you, but I'm not so sure about that.

I'm sorry if I come off a little bitter.

Then the shot.

I take it. I'm always the lucky guy.

It tears through the sleeve of my jacket and burns into my arm like a trail of fire. The impact of it spins me a quarter turn. Maybe. Or maybe it's the surprise that turns me, or some kind of knowing that I wouldn't believe until just now.

It feels like the bullet.

Now that I'm turned, I'm staring down the muzzle of an American Browning. Trouble is, the boy on the ground behind it's not an American. Not even close.

I'm dead, only I don't know it yet.

It might take me forty years or so to figure it out.

Maybe you're wondering at this point, like, how did a Jap boy lay hold of an American-made weapon, or how did he happen to miss the Tokyo Express. Here you have the advantage of me. They are very good questions, and I'd like to wonder them myself, but I'm busy dying.

Everything after this happens in slow motion.

A round leaves the muzzle of the gun, aimed at my forehead. I watch it fly.

I send a short message to my feet. It's garbled in panic. I'm afraid when it finally gets there, they won't understand.

I decide it doesn't matter, because whatever my feet do with the information will be better than what they're doing now.

I wonder how long a message takes to travel from a brain to a pair of feet. I never had to wonder before, because the world has never moved so slowly, never broken down into such obvious and specific and carefully planned sequences.

I decide that if it's longer than a round of ammunition takes to travel from the muzzle of a Browning M-2 to a forehead some thirty feet away, the answer will come up moot.

Then I decide the bullet is winning.

I'm sure you think there isn't time to know all this in the flight time of the bullet, but excuse me, you're alive. You'll have to trust me. I've been places you think you haven't.

The best news I can give you is that it doesn't hurt. Death never does. Sometimes the moments leading up to it can be painful, but the dying is always easy.

I feel it as impact.

It feels, actually, like an inside job. Like some pressure within my head causes it to explode.

It throws me over backwards.

I'm flying back through the air now, thinking I will land. Because, you see, I still think I'm alive, and that the old laws of inevitability will have some meaning for me.

I have to land.

I don't.

Because somewhere on the way down there ceases to be Walter, so who is this person I think must land?

Then I sit up.

Am I confusing you? Well, I'm sorry, but at this point there's no reason for you to be any clearer on all this than I am.

Okay, here, I'll sketch it out for you as best I can: Somebody sits up, and it's me, but it's not Walter. And this body on the ground does not sit up. Because that's Walter, and he's dead.

Better? Good. I knew I could clear things up.

Ordinarily, I think, souls are not commonly known to sit up. They like to float, fly, that sort of thing. They are not often found acting bodylike. I think my soul is experiencing a moment of confusion. Some sort of final identity crisis.

I look around at the body. Who was this poor fool again? What on earth happened to the rest of his head? I can't imagine.

I watch Andrew as he tries to pull the body to cover. Watch him risk his life for an empty.

It hits me, what I am. What I can do. What I don't have to do. There's a special kind of freedom to that moment. I could never in a million years describe it to you.

I watch Andrew pretend this boy with half a head will make it, watch him wade through a line of fire, unhit, empty body in tow.

I see his guilt and rage and pain, not just now, but stretched to infinity. It's not a disturbing image. In fact, it's strangely beautiful. It's something he needs to do, and even the most painful aspects of it—especially the most painful aspects— are just exquisite.

Me, I'm free.

I take off flying.

Over the jungle, which no longer stinks or threatens. Over the tops of millions of palm trees. Over a blue-green ocean too perfect to host violence.

Okay.

Now we can get on with it.

Now we are at the beginning.

It makes no difference whether you believe all this or you don't. It not only makes no difference to me, but to anything. Things don't wait for you to believe them. They happen.

God is not Tinkerbell.

He does what he does whether you clap your hands or hide behind the comfort of your disbelief.

Besides, you know all this. You just forgot.

CHAPTER TWO

Michael

At 6:00 A.M. he arrives at the first greenhouse, breathes the satisfying aroma. He weaves between tall rows in the dim light, reverent as if in church.

He checks first the tallest plants, those whose uppermost leaves might press against the opaque roof, leaving an imprint of the familiar five-leaf pattern visible from the air.

It's nearly harvest. Flyby season. This is the season of antacids, of intestines that freeze at the sound of a motor. Any motor. The season when you bargain with that God you never really believed in, swear on your life that safe passage through this season is all you'll ever need, all you'll ever ask for. No more favors. Next year you'll grow organics in the greenhouses. Swear. How many seasons Michael has done this particular dance, well, at least on this morning he really doesn't stop to consider.

For a gentle hour he thins leaves away from the developing buds. Like children, they need light and fresh air.

Spiders have woven intricate webs in corners and between long stems, and the morning dew hangs on each strand of these creations, making them appear somehow more beautiful and more important than anything has a right to be. The soil mashes softly under his feet, a comfort.

He moves to the second greenhouse, raises his eyes, and everything changes. The view, the mood, everything. It's instantly a different world. He shouts a blast of his rage.

"Oh, shit! Damn it, goddamn it!"

He runs to the third, the fourth. His eyes scan the tops of every plant. The valuable, bud-laden tops. Or in any case, he examines the spot where these tops should have been, where they had been just yesterday.

Half the crop has been spared.

Half the crop has been stolen.

At this moment, Michael would attest that his glass is at least half empty.

Dennis, who should be down in the kiwi field, comes at a run.

"What the hell is wrong with you, Michael? Shut up, man, want the neighbors to call the sheriff?"

Michael says nothing, just points. Dennis raises his eyes to half their harvestable plants. Sees what Michael has already seen. That each of their valuable tops has been broken off in the night.

"Oh, crap, man. We been ripped off."

"No shit, Dennis."

"Well, at least I said it quietly."

· ★ ·

Dennis hands it over gingerly, more like Michael might hurt it than like it might hurt Michael.

"You know how to use one of these things?"

"Hell, no. Never touched a gun in my life."

"Well, let me show you, then."

He straps the deer rifle to the trunk of the avocado tree, using both of their belts.

The early evening dusk feels warm and strange, as if something other than just nature is afoot. Then again, Michael is stoned, so it's hard to judge things by how they seem.

"Okay, now watch. Safety off. Trigger. Got it? The only way you can shoot is up. I'll come out and finish the job, only by then they'll be gone. I warn you, man, this thing has got a report on it."

"Huh?"

"It'll slap back on your ear like a steel spike."

"I don't get it."

"It's loud, man."

"Oh. Good."

Dennis shakes his head a few times. Then he picks his way

back over the wooden bridge, leaving Michael alone in the moonlight.

Michael takes stock of his supplies. Rifle. Bottle of wine. Sleeping bag. Flashlight. Three joints. Matches.

He fires up a joint, draws deeply, then takes a long pull off the bottle. The light of a hunter's moon throws shadows of a hundred avocado trees across the side of the hill. A warm Santa Ana wind rolls down, shaking the steady walls of his cover. The sound is what registers most. The shushing noise of the blowing leaves, like running water. Like distant applause.

An avocado tree makes good camp, he's learned, its long branches brushing the ground. If the intruders come back for the rest of the crop, he'll see them clearly. They won't see him. Only a hundred trees. Which one holds the armed farmer? They won't know, so they'll run.

He delights in the mental vision, three or four high school kids, tripping over each other like the Marx Brothers or Keystone Kops. Rolling down the hill one on top of the other. Running for their lives as far as they know.

Next year, he'll come out to guard earlier, before they lose half the crop.

No, there won't be a next year.

Next year they'll grow organics in the greenhouses. Good money in that. Not this good, but you won't have to lose your stomach to the sound of a plane or a helicopter. Better for the spirit. For the moment, he has forgotten having formulated this resolution in the past.

He fires up the second joint on the heels of the first. Chain-smoking. A sense of peace settles over him, starting in his belly, radiating out along his arms and legs. He feels good. He's not afraid.

He is also not sleepy.

This is a problem. This not being sleepy, it needs to be dealt with. His senses feel fully alive. In the house, this would not be such a problem. But what does one do for entertainment under an avocado tree in the dark?

He unstraps the rifle, shines the flashlight on it, checks the safety. Holds it in his hands, just to feel the weight, the heft of it. Maybe he just wants to know how it feels to hold a gun. Maybe the curiosity goes deeper than that, but if so, he doesn't recognize the place it begins. But the heft of it in his hands, that he recognizes. That's a familiar feeling. Which might seem strange to him, if he weren't too loaded to notice when a thing doesn't fit.

He decides to begin a marching patrol, which he performs with the rifle angled on his shoulder, like a proud soldier on parade day.

He stops on the little bridge, his senses pulling in the rushing creek, hearing it, smelling it.

He snaps the rifle down, satisfied with the rap its stock makes on the wooden boards, and stands at ease.

Then he does something which seems strangely natural at the time, and which he thinks nothing at all about. He reviews the military manual of arms, calling the commands himself in a crisp whisper, a gentle drill sergeant.

"Ten—hut! Right shoulder . . . harms! Port . . . harms!"

He swings the rifle in accordance with each command,

with never a doubt or question. Each move seems to hold its own sense of confidence. Each move is a living thing, a thing with a separate will, able to act on its own.

He shifts his hands from balance to stock, spins the trigger housing away from his body, sets the barrel on his shoulder, drops his left hand smartly to his side.

The only glitch comes as he fails to find the balance just behind the trigger housing, as expected.

"Funny gun," he says under his breath, although it's the only gun he has ever known.

"Parade . . . rest." He opens his stance to hip distance, sets the rifle butt on the ground beside his right foot, muzzle tilted forward, left hand behind his back.

"Fix . . . bayonets!" His left hand grasps the muzzle, he brings the rifle slightly left across him. His right hand reaches around to his belt, and he comes up empty. In more ways than one.

It breaks the spell, turns him back into a young pot farmer on a wooden bridge in the moonlight, touching a weapon for the first time. Turns him back to a man who has never learned the thing he just practiced, who can't explain what he seems able to do. Caught in an act that feels natural and yet makes no logical sense.

Michael feels chastened in a manner that remains difficult to understand.

Gun dangling from his hand, he picks his way back to his camp by the greenhouses. As he often does when faced with confusing questions, he cuts a deal with himself to never ask them again.

· ★ ·

The first night following harvest he breaks the deal. He sits on the bare floor of the half-finished house, cross-legged, watches by lantern as Dennis hunches mesmerized over his Ouija board.

Dennis takes on a special concentration in front of the board. He leans forward, his body curved into the shape of a letter *C,* his brow furrowed. Michael thinks Dennis looks older in front of the Ouija board. He also feels he sees what Dennis doesn't see—that the Ouija board user is fooling himself. His fingers can push that little pointer without conscious intention. A person can just sit alone at that board and make all his own inner thoughts come true. A classic version of seeing what you want to see.

"I never believed in those things," Michael says.

"Fine. Whatever. Ouija board works if you believe in it or if you don't."

It makes an eerie kind of sense to Michael, in his stoned state.

"Anyway, it scares me, thinking you could, like, talk to a spirit or something."

"How can it scare you if you don't believe it?"

"Oh. Well, if I believed it, it would scare me."

Dennis looks up. Furrows his brow even more deeply at Michael, shakes his head. Michael has broken his concentration now, ruined the moment. He does these things when he's stoned. Sometimes he does these things when he's not.

Dennis gets up and goes upstairs to bed, leaving the Ouija board sitting on the floor.

Michael stares at the board for what feels like an hour.

More likely it's only a very long few minutes. He wishes Dennis had put it away. Now he's staring at it and feeling as if it's staring at him. And to put it away, he'd have to touch it. He's not sure he wants to touch it.

Maybe he believes more than he cares to admit. He pushes the thought away again.

Maybe he is more interested in the board than usual because he has a pressing question. This is an unfamiliar sensation. Michael has made it through twenty-one years with few, if any, pressing questions. The fewer the better as far as he is concerned.

He decides that a half-bottle of wine might ease his paranoia, and he tries it. It seems to work. The board looks more like a friend, someone who would happily answer a simple question.

He sets the board on his lap and asks it to explain the part about the rifle drill.

He is able to do this without much fear, because he feels comfortably sure that it won't.

The pointer jerks against the tips of his fingers, just as he had so hoped it wouldn't. It moves under his hands like something living, and takes him along for the ride.

Much as he has always believed that the user must do the moving, he can't imagine that he is pushing. It doesn't feel that way. It feels sure, therefore foreign. And he doesn't know what answer he wants, can't even guess at one, so where would his subconscious send the pointer? He can't imagine what he might tell himself that he doesn't already know.

The pointer spells out this message.

HI MICHAEL

He freezes in a wave of goose bumps, and his scalp tingles. He thinks of throwing the board off his lap, but the pointer keeps going, spelling out a long, rambling message.

DONT BE AFRAID ITS ONLY YOU

"Me?" he says out loud, listening to the ringing of blood in his ears.

Nothing moves.

He asks whoever he might be talking to, if indeed he's talking to somebody, if he knows the answer to the puzzle. He asks it a second time, out loud. "Do you know where that drill stuff came from?"

The pointer shoots to the word.

YES

"How did I know how to do all that?"

Quickly, steadily, it spells out, BECAUSE I KNOW.

Michael chews on that for a moment, wishing for a reason not to continue. *Because I know.* Does that explain anything?

"Why should I know what you know?" Whoever "you" are, he thinks, but doesn't say.

BECAUSE IM YOU

"So your name is Michael?"

NO

"So, in what way are you me?"

"What'd you say, Mike?" The voice is real, loud, cutting.

Michael screams, throws the board and pointer into the air.

Dennis stands in the doorway, looking amused. Michael has one hand on his chest and is trying to restart his breathing. He can feel his heart pound against that hand.

"Dennis, holy shit, don't do that."

"Hey, d'you get something, man?"

"Maybe. No. I don't know."

He pushes the board away with his foot and pretends he'll go to sleep.

CHAPTER THREE

Walter

Did you think I was gone?

No chance of that. If death was the end of me, this story would be over.

Nobody in this story is going anywhere without me. They don't know enough, don't know where to go.

I don't mean to insult these people, sounding like I'm the only one who knows anything. I mean, these people are my friends. It's just that, when you're alive . . . Oh, boy. How do I say this without offending everybody? When you're alive, you don't know squat. It's like being lost in the woods. You don't see the woods, and you don't really know where you are. It's like you just see the trees right around you, and you have no idea what part of the forest it is, or how it fits in with the rest of the forest. If you're walking around trying to get found, you probably don't even know if you've seen these particular trees before. No perspective, you know? No overview.

I guess I sound prejudiced against the living, and maybe in some ways I am. When you've done both and you know it, it's hard not to see what's what.

I will say this, though. A few living people have some kind of breakthrough knowing. For lack of a better expression. It's like some part of them knows the whole forest, and every now and then they can operate out of that part of themselves. But they can't do it all the time, and they could never explain it to you.

So even though it has limited uses, I still have to give credit where credit is due and admit that some living people are knowers.

Mary Ann used to be that way. That's why the little incident in the backseat of my dad's Ford just before I shipped out. I didn't see it like that at the time. I wasn't much of a knower myself, back then.

But she knew I wasn't coming back.

I wonder if she's still got that. I hope so. It'll help a lot, if she does. But it's a funny thing, knowing. It's the first thing to get knocked out of you. Life has a way of finding that part of you and taking it back.

I'll tell you who used to be a great knower was Bobby. You

won't meet him, because he's dead. Really dead, not stuck like me. He was a buddy of Andrew's and mine on the island. Good guy, Bobby.

Not long after we land, he goes off and buys a native hooker for the four of us. Yeah, that was a good example of what I'm talking about. That was a knowing thing, and maybe I saw it that way when it happened, even though I was obviously alive at the time.

There were four of us that were real close on the island. The four musketeers, that's what we called ourselves. Me, Andrew, Bobby, and Jay.

Anyway, the thing with the hooker. This is where I am right now. I feel guilty calling her that, even though it's what she is, because she looks about sixteen, and I keep imagining that if the Japs and the GIs had never landed, she might've just been a girl like any other—like your daughter or your sister.

Anyway, she isn't.

She costs Bobby his gold pinky ring. That pays for all four of us. Nice gesture, only I feel pretty inclined to give it a miss. It's one of those things, though, you have to take into account what your musketeers will say, so I go in for my share.

She's lying on Bobby's jacket in the dusk, in the jungle. Wearing nothing more than that ring on her middle finger. She's holding her hand out at arm's length, like to admire the look. I know how many guys have been in to see her already, but she doesn't look like she knows. She looks like she forgot to notice. I'm standing there in front of her, and all she can do is look at the ring.

She has this vulnerability about her that I think I'm supposed to find exciting, only it doesn't work on me. Lots of things that are supposed to work on guys don't work on me. I hope I never find out why.

It makes me feel sad.

But I do it anyway, so I can honestly say I did. It's a present, you know? It's a guy thing.

The whole time, she's looking over my shoulder at her outstretched hand. At least she's honest about what's important to her.

Anyway, I don't take up too much of her time, so I guess I shouldn't feel too bad.

Then, when it's over, I have a laugh to myself, thinking how Andrew calls this Anticlimax Island, except for different reasons.

Not that the first time was any great shakes, or lasted much longer, but at least I knew my girl was there because she liked me. Now that I think about it, though, I had to give Mary Ann a ring, too.

So, anyway. About the knowing thing. So I go back to Bobby and I say, "Hey, thanks, buddy, that was just the ticket."

Pretty much lying.

He says, "Well, it's like this, Crow." That's what they call me, Crow. He says, "We're going back to the hill tomorrow, and you just never know." He says, "If we don't get some now, maybe we won't be able to later. And you got to get you some at least once before you die." He says, "Damn shame to have to go to heaven and tell Saint Peter you forgot to live while you had the chance."

Well, this kind of gets my attention, because how do you suppose he got it in his head that I never did?

So I go back to Andrew, and I say, "What the hell, buddy, did you tell Bobby I was a virgin?"

Andrew says, "Hey, we're all in the same boat, it's nothing you need to be ashamed of."

Because, you see, I still hadn't gotten around to telling him about Mary Ann.

More on that later. That's a whole thing. Don't even get me started on that now.

So not two days down the pike we're charging a cave. Three of us guys go running in at a time, in waves, and I trip over something in the dark and go flying. Whatever it is, I figure it must've saved my life, for the moment, because before I can get up and get back into combat, it's all over. Score one for the U.S. of A.

Hutch comes in with a big, battery-powered light so we can evacuate our dead and wounded.

So then I see what I tripped over. Bobby.

Run through with a bayonet. Eyes like glass, staring up at the cave ceiling. Staring at nothing.

And my first thought—call it sick if you will—is, At least he got laid first.

And then my second thought is, How'd he know? Who told him it was time?

And then my third thought is that I'm going to throw up and I do.

See, the point of that story is that Bobby was a knower. I wonder sometimes if he was always like that, or if it was just because he was so close. When you're that close to the moment you're going to die, it gets to be like a thin curtain between the two things, the living thing and the dying one, and you can see a lot if you try.

But Mary Ann is living a long life, and she knew things young. Some people do.

Michael, now he presents a challenge. He knows nothing, and he doesn't even mind that. He's not even paying attention. I know I talk about him like he isn't me. And we all know he is. But still. He's going to take some working on.

But then, I've got all the time in the world, right? No buses to catch. No pressing engagements. What better have I got to do?

CHAPTER FOUR

Michael

Not long after midnight, in that free zone, the state that brings dream symbols that surprise the dreamer because he thinks he's awake, Michael slips into a sort of enforced darkness.

His dream carries no visual impressions, only sound and feeling.

He feels clammy, cool stone walls, rough against his hands and shoulders, hears the sounds of struggle. Muffled shouts, some in English, some not.

A body slams against him, drives him into the moist, mossy

stone. He feels the pain of impact, the dampness of the wall against his back. Feels the breath rush out of him in an involuntary sigh.

Then a voice, vaguely familiar, shouts something he understands. It's a warning. A grave, sudden, hopeless warning.

It says, "Whit!"

He knows this warning is meant for Andrew, because that's what they call Andrew. Whit.

The next sound Michael hears is that of a man run through with a bayonet.

It's a subtle sound, but distinct. A grunt. A rush of air. A little hard to describe but he knows it. You only need to hear a thing like that once. It will stay with you.

He sits up in bed and shouts Andrew's name, startled awake as in a falling dream, sure that he is too late.

Seconds later, Dennis comes running.

"What the hell's the matter with you, man?"

"Oh. I think I might have had a dream."

"Might have? Who the hell is Andrew?"

"I don't know."

Dennis shakes his head and stumbles back to bed. On his way through the door he mumbles this over his shoulder: "You been weird lately, man."

· ★ ·

Three days later, sometime near dusk, Dennis finds him in the corn. Dennis is walking purposefully. Too purposefully, Michael thinks. Michael bends back into his weeding, sensing a message coming, knowing it's a message he doesn't want delivered.

Dennis says, "You been playing with my Ouija board again."

Michael feels strangely caught, as if this simple act were illegal. "Yeah? So?"

"You got somebody on the line."

"What makes you say?"

"Well, I was using it just now. And guess what it said to me? 'Where's Michael?'"

Michael stares, cold and shaken; then he laughs and shakes his head.

"Real funny, Dennis."

"I'm not joking, man."

Michael knows he isn't joking, knows it from his voice, refuses to look at his face, refuses to seek confirmation.

He swallows hard.

"That stuff scares the shit out of me, Dennis. I am never going near that board again. I can't even get too high anymore, or it makes me paranoid."

"It's not that big a deal, man. When somebody latches on to you like that, it usually means they need help."

"Help?" he shouts. "Help with what, Dennis? Income tax? Does he want me to help him change a tire? Exactly what does a spirit need that I could help with?" He finishes in a drawn-out yell that scratches his throat and makes him cough.

Dennis stares him down, unfazed. "Why don't you ask him?"

"Yeah, sure."

"Then *I* will."

Michael watches him go. He stays in place, his feet rooted to the spot, heavy and useless. It's the way they feel in the recurring dream, when he most needs to run.

He wants to stop Dennis, to stop the process, but he knows you can't overpower something that has no physical form.

· ★ ·

Over a month passes in a silence that extends even to Michael's dreams. If he dreams at all, upon waking each image is conveniently gone.

His life retakes the comfortable landmarks of the way it had always been. No pressing questions.

Then late one night, Dennis comes into his room and shakes him awake.

"I just had a long talk with your friend."

Michael sits up, rubs his eyes, feels his scratchy trace of beard. Dennis has broken an essential—though unspoken—pact, waking him out of a sound sleep. In the air hangs a sense that this had better be good. Also that it had better stop being cryptic, preferably now.

"What friend?"

"His name is Walter."

"I don't have any friends named Walter."

"You do now."

It hits him then, a steel bat of words, and he doesn't need or want to ask more questions.

"I wish you hadn't pursued this, Dennis."

"It wasn't my idea. Look, if you care, he told me what he's after."

"After?"

"What he needs from you."

"Needs from me?"

"Wake up, man."

Is he asleep? Is that the only problem?

"Okay," he says, listening to the tremor in his own voice with detached interest. "What does he want from me?"

"He wants you to find Andrew." The name sinks through Michael's stomach like a man in quicksand. The more you struggle, the faster you sink. "You must be real connected to this guy, or you wouldn't have had that dream."

Michael swallows in a tight way he can hear as well as feel. "I don't want to have anything to do with this." He knows in some part of himself that it's too late. He already has plenty to do with it. But he wants to live in the other small part, the part that believes it isn't true.

"Okay, fine, man, I only said I'd give you the message."

"Don't be my messenger, Dennis."

Dennis leaves without further comment.

· ★ ·

Michael lies awake for three or four hours, knowing somehow that when he sleeps the weeks of respite will be over. And of course he's right. Without even knowing he was about to drop off, he falls into a nightmare.

In his dream he sets off behind four other soldiers through grass as tall as his head. It cuts like a thousand hacksaws as they push through it, leaving jagged lacerations on his face, wrists, hands.

Mosquitoes bite into his neck, he swats them. A cold sweat breaks out on his face, because he knows the mosquitoes carry malaria.

Now he wades chest-deep through a swamp, holding the waistband of the man in front of him for purchase. The swamp stinks like death; the whole island stinks. The rain comes down in sheets, turning the dry land to soupy mud before they can reach it. He pulls and strains but can thrust his legs forward only two or three inches at a time. They become weak and shaky with the strain, but he can't stop. His legs are ready to fold underneath him, but he can't stop.

He sees the small, cold green eyes of a crocodile and shouts in warning. The front man shoots it, but it isn't dead, only angry. It snaps onto a boy three paces in front of him. The boy screams, and his blood spills, bright red, to blend with the churning mud.

Michael startles awake and decides not to go back to sleep. He holds to that decision for nearly forty-eight hours. No one can hold it forever.

· ★ ·

Michael dreams himself at the mouth of a cave, running.

He knows he needs to go back, but he can't. He won't.

Say Hutch, he thinks as he bolts into the blinding sunlight. Yell for Hutch.

He opens his mouth, but no sound comes out. Hutch lobs a mortar round at him. Michael wakes up on the floor.

He makes it almost seventy-two hours without sleep this time, then begins to hallucinate, which is worse.

· ★ ·

Dennis finds him three weeks later, a quarter mile up the creek bank, trying to keep his eyes open. He finds him easily, because Michael is playing his saxophone. The music sounds low and mournful, though not as good as it otherwise might. The music is thin and worn down, too.

"Tired of fighting a war, man?"

"What do you mean, 'war'? Why did you say 'war'?"

"You don't know how much you yell out in your sleep. I never seen you look this bad off, man. Why don't you stop fighting this? I know it seems weird, scary maybe, but what could be worse than this?"

It may only be due to sleep deprivation, but Michael feels this makes a degree of sense.

· ★ ·

Michael props the Ouija board on his lap and steadies his shaking hands.

"Will things get better if I find Andrew?" he asks out loud.

The pointer jumps to the word.

YES

"How the hell do I find him? I don't even know his last name."

Alive under his fingers, it spells slowly.

WHITTAKER

He stops, breathes. Great, he thinks. Now I have a name. A real name, maybe of a real person. It seems to Michael that now there is no going back. He wishes he had stopped before now.

"I'm sure there's lots of Andrew Whittakers," he says, wanting some point on which to argue. "How do I know when I've got the right one?"

HE KNEW WALTER CROWLEY

This name rings familiar. Did he dream that, too?

"Are you sure this Andrew is still alive?"

YES

"What if I find him, what the hell do I do with him?"

YOULL KNOW

"Fine, I'll know. Great."

He puts aside the board, stands too fast, almost passes out. His stomach feels weak and empty, like he's losing a bout with the flu. He drops immediately into bed and sleeps over sixteen hours, in peace.

· ★ ·

Michael wakes in the late morning, dresses in clothes from the day before, and unshowered and unshaven, leaves the house.

He drives two and a half hours to the Santa Barbara library, the closest library that stocks phone books for every state.

He makes a pencil list of twenty-two Andrew Whittakers, then the library closes for the day.

He sleeps in his van, a heavy, dreamless sleep, wakes feeling rested, and begins the task again.

He is still unshaven, dressed in day-before-yesterday's clothes, and a couple of the librarians have begun to eye him strangely.

Despite their lack of support, he lists sixty-two more addresses.

CHAPTER FIVE

Mary Ann

Mary Ann wakes to find herself fully engaged in a state of knowing. She doesn't yet know what she knows, but the intensity of the feeling surprises her.

She hasn't felt it this strongly since 1942.

Since then, there've been little things. The phone would ring, and she would know who was calling. Sometimes before the first ring. Or she and Andrew would watch football on Sunday, and just prior to the snap she'd think, He'll throw an interception, and sure enough, some grinning linebacker would pick off the pass.

So it's not that the knowing was gone, exactly. She did not

convince herself that it was gone. Only that it seemed confined to the insignificant.

This, however, matters.

Last time anything mattered this much, it was Walter, always Walter. He's not coming back, he's been hit, he's afraid, he's gone.

Now, with Walter gone forty years, it seems hard to imagine that the knowing centers around him. It feels like it does, though.

She climbs out of bed and pushes the moment away, forces it to evaporate like a dream upon waking. She has gardening to do. Housework. Real things that can be seen and touched and talked about. Real things should rightfully come first.

The other is just an indistinct feeling.

Something's going to happen. That's all she knows for sure.

· ★ ·

Three days later she comes in from her garden to find Andrew crouched over his little desk, sorting the mail.

She washes up at the kitchen sink, then comes back to the living room to see him squinting at a photocopied letter. She sits on the couch, tries not to look or pry, hoping patience will bring the answer. What's so distressing, so worthy of concern?

When you know someone well, you gather a great deal from his body language. She sees that the letter Andrew is reading has caused his shoulders to pull up and forward. It's put him in that mood she knows, the one where he'd like to snap at someone over something blissfully unrelated. At times like this he welcomes the chance.

When he's spent almost five minutes on the same sheet of paper, she asks straight out.

"What is it, dear? Some kind of problem?"

Once it would have been unlike her to intervene in anything that troubled him, to even suggest he might need assistance. Since he retired, though, he seems more lost in minor details, more stranded in the smallest concerns. Part of her finds this disturbing. Another part of her feels it has chinked away at the wall between them. Not quite leveled the playing field, but made strides in that direction.

"I don't know. Somebody asking if I knew Walter Crowley. Doesn't say why, though."

It always strikes her as a blow to find her knowing correct, even though it always is, it always has been, and its rightness should logically come as no surprise.

"May I see it, dear?"

He holds the letter back over his shoulder, and she takes it out of his hand.

April 19, 1982

Dear Mr. Whittaker,

 I am writing to many Andrew Whittakers in hope of finding a particular one.

 Thank you for taking a moment of your time.

*Did you once know a Walter Crowley? Maybe
dating back to the war years? If so, I'd very much
appreciate a response.*
    Thank you.
    Yours sincerely,
      Michael Steeb

On the third read-through she realizes she must be taking
more time with the letter than Andrew did.

He says, "Just throw it away when you're done."

"Throw it away? You can't do that, Andrew. He's looking
for someone who knew Walter."

"Fine, then you write to him."

"Why are you acting like this?"

He keeps his face turned away, but she imagines his expression from experience, brow creased, eyes shaded over,
blank.

"None of his business, who I knew."

"You don't know that. You don't even know who it is."

"Exactly the point I'm trying to make you see." His voice
comes up, he turns to her, half rises out of his chair. Once it
might have seemed a formidable gesture. She wonders if it's
her imagination, or if old age has made him smaller.

"Maybe it's important. You don't know it's none of his
business until you know why he's asking."

"Until I know why he's asking, I want nothing to do with
him. You want to write back, write back. You answer his
questions. Don't tell me anything about it."

As he heads for the door and his afternoon walk, she notices his limp seems worse than usual.

WALTER'S PURPLE HEART

April 23, 1982

Dear Mr. Steeb,
 Both my husband and I knew Walter very well.
 My husband seems reluctant to discuss it with you.
 Maybe it would help if you could give us more information as to what your interest in the situation might be.
 Meanwhile, I will soften him up as best I can.
 Sincerely,
  Mrs. Andrew Whittaker

Mary Ann folds the thin sheet of stationery and slides it into its envelope, carefully copying Mr. Steeb's address from his letter.

She notices a fine layer of dust on the little oak writing desk. So much dust gathers. She has to see to it daily. On any other day she would have dusted by now. It feels good somehow to have broken from routine.

Then, knowing full well what she's doing, she lets her eyes come up to the portrait of Walter on the desktop. It's always there, but this time she sees it. She has tried to see it often. It's become a mental exercise, a battle against diminishing returns.

She would look at it several times a day in the forties, trying to see it the way she once had. To really see it, not just register it as something memorized, too familiar. Then she tried once a month or so. Now only on special occasions she will stare at the photo and try to imagine some animation to the features.

It never works. It's too damn familiar. There are only just so many times you can look at something before you no longer see it.

Sometimes Mary Ann thinks that if she had known that, she would have put the picture away in a drawer and rationed her viewing time.

But it's too late now, and besides, she knows she could never have done that.

CHAPTER SIX

Walter

If there's one thing I learned in my all-too-short, barely twenty-one-year stint as Walter, it's this. Any decent man has to feel something for a woman who dearly loves him. Gratitude, if he can muster nothing else.

But for Mary Ann, gratitude didn't seem like nearly enough. I liked her a lot, but that was never going to do. I had to listen to the guys in the locker room after track and try to duplicate all that lust in my own life. It's a losing game. You either feel a thing or you don't.

I meet Mary Ann in our senior year, the day she transfers to our school from upstate New York.

She sits in the bleachers after class, watching me and Andrew run track. She doesn't watch the other guys run track. Just me and Andrew. I don't notice that at first, but the other guys do. They go on about it.

I figure she's there for Andrew, because he has so much stuff I don't. Stuff. You know. Usually I'm good with words, but that's a tough one. I'm not sure how to find the perfect word for that. Like he knows who he is. Like he's brave enough for anything, like everything is under control.

He figures she's there for me, says it's because I'm better looking. I'm surprised. I'm not sure I knew I was better looking. I start looking in the mirror more to see if that's true.

Now Mary Ann, she is definitely something to look at. Something about real red hair, carrot-red, with a halo of sun coming through it, and skin like porcelain.

I think, What a pretty girl, but it's more like just a thought in my head. I could never figure out how to pull that all the way down into my loins and make it sing. Other guys don't need to figure that out at all. It's like something they were born with. Me, I don't know. I'm not so sure about me.

After practice I ask her what she thinks of Ocean City. She says she likes it a whole lot better now that someone's taken the time to be friendly.

Now that doesn't seem like much, does it? But it's like lighting the fuse on a keg of gunpowder. Everything that follows is inevitable.

So after that the whole thing takes on a life of its own. I don't mind, because as best I can figure, it's supposed to happen this way. But it feels off, like something that's always happening a few yards away.

She hangs around me as much as she can, the guys start poking me in the ribs, asking if I've made it to second base. They say I'm a lucky guy, I got a pretty girl, I should hold on tight, so I do. When I'm around them, I see it through their eyes and it feels right. So I talk about it a lot. Keep it real. Other guys talk about their girls a lot, too, but it might be different. How do I know? Maybe I'm normal and I just don't know how normal feels.

Sometimes I study the look in her eyes when she looks at me, and wonder if it's something you can learn, or if you have to be born knowing it.

And believe me, I have plenty of time to wonder. From senior year of high school until I ship out. We're talking three years she's waited for something to break. Keep somebody waiting that long for an answer, the answer better be good.

So before I leave for basic training I'm supposed to propose. Nobody says that straight out, but it's funny how you know these things. We go out on dates, or take walks on the boardwalk near sunset, and I can hear myself not ask the question. It leaves a big hole in that place where it should have been. You find yourself staring at the hole, not knowing where else to look.

I don't know what I would have done if she hadn't forced my hand three days before we were to ship out.

Me and Andrew enlisted, you see, so we could go on the buddy system. Well, actually we did it because he said we were going to, that's why. But the buddy system was a big incentive. Damned if I was going out there all alone.

So just before we're to go, I take her out on one last date, the one that'll have to do for a while. I borrow my dad's Ford, get all dressed up in a suit and tie, and we go dancing. That's what my dad said I should do. He said I could be away a long time, and that's a hard time for a girl, home waiting. He had no idea.

Anyway, that's where I am. On the boardwalk with my girl. Kind of rolling along arm in arm. Just out of the dance and on our way back to my dad's car. Kind of nursing that sense that this night has to be special. I think that's what got us in trouble. That sense that something had to happen that was bigger and better than anything that had happened before.

It's Mary Ann's idea to go park. It's a long drive out to where people our age park, but if that's what she wants . . . Well, you know. It's like a last wish before her guy goes off to war. You don't just say no to a thing like that.

So we're out there, and we're kissing, more than we've really kissed before, and it feels different. And she has one of my shirt buttons undone and her hands inside my shirt and it feels nice.

Then she says, "Let's get in the backseat."

I'm not so sure about this.

So I say, "Hey, Mary Ann, I'm not so sure about this."

She seems a little hurt and disappointed. She wants to know why not.

I say, "I don't think I'm the kind of guy who asks a girl to do that."

"You didn't," she says. "I asked you." She says, "I know what I'm doing, I'm a big girl. I can make my own decisions about these things."

I say, "Sometimes what feels like a good decision in the heat of the moment can feel like a big regret later on."

I hate to say it, but I think I accidentally borrowed that line from my dad.

She says, about three or four different ways, that she can never be made to regret what we're about to do.

I say, "Look. Nobody likes to think in these terms, but what if I don't come home? Then you'll have to marry someone else, and then you'll wish you hadn't done this."

I've been doing this a lot lately. With just about everybody I know. Dropping the idea that I might not come back. And it goes over very badly. Everything goes quiet, and I get these awful looks. Which I really don't understand, because we all know it's a possibility. So why can't we say it out loud?

Mary Ann is different. This is one of the times I know she's different. That I know that I have something in her that's better than what most other people have.

She looks that one right in the eye.

She says, "You know, I think that's a big part of why we should. Because what if you never come home? In that case," she says, "I won't do either of those things you just mentioned. I won't marry anybody else, and I won't regret tonight."

I am now officially out of excuses.

So she climbs over into the backseat, and I say, "You know I'm still not that—" but before I can say the word "sure," she grabs me by my tie and pulls me over. Well, not literally, but she pulls hard, and it seems in my best interests to follow my tie.

Even now, in the backseat, I'm still not sure this is such a good idea, but then she starts touching me in some ways that go beyond anything we've done before, and after a while I'm not sure it's such a bad idea, either.

You know how these things take on their own momentum. Then a minute later it's all over, good idea or not.

I just know she must be disappointed, but she says she's not, and since I really don't know what makes it enjoyable for a girl, I can't be sure she's lying. But there's something embarrassing about it, in a deep way. It's not a good moment.

She wants to cuddle and be close. I have this clammy feeling in my stomach, and I want to go home.

I want to turn on the dome light and see if we left a stain on the cloth inserts of my dad's upholstery. It's all I can think about. But she's all caught up in love, and I can't do a thing like that to her. So I hold her, wondering how long a stain takes to set in.

Then I take her home. How do you say good night in this situation? You have to kiss your girl in a way that'll last all through the war. If you come home. Or forever if you don't. And all the time you're trying to figure out how such a thing is possible, you can just feel that stain setting in. Talk about pressure.

I do my best.

Later that night I work on it, out in the driveway with a flashlight and a can of spot remover. The stain still isn't gone. So I convince myself it will look better dry, and I go to bed.

I say a prayer. I say, Please, God, don't let him notice. Bad enough that I took the car to Atlantic City and put a dent in it. Now this. Or if he notices, please let him think somebody spilled some food or something.

It's a real dumb prayer, and I picture God laughing when he hears it, because no one would dare take food into Dad's '39 Ford. Not even God.

But I stand by it anyway, and swear that if he just does that for me, it's the last thing I'll ever ask. People do that all the time, though, and they always ask for more later. And if *I've* noticed that, you have to figure God's on to how that happens. But really, at the time it feels sincere.

Then it hits me that Mary Ann might get pregnant, so I ask to make one slight amendment.

Don't let him notice the stain, don't let Mary Ann get pregnant. That's everything in the world that's important to me. I'll never ask another special favor.

He doesn't outright refuse the deal, despite what he undoubtedly knows.

It occurs to me that I might have saved a prayer or two for later, what with going off to war and all, but right now I can't believe that anything could be scarier than this.

I borrow forty-five dollars from my dad so I can buy Mary Ann a nice ring, not a cheap one, so she can show it off and all her friends'll know I did right by her. That I wasn't a bad choice.

I promise to pay him back out of my twenty-one-dollar-a-month military pay. He'll hold me to it. If you don't believe it, you don't know my dad. Probably if I die overseas before the debt is paid, I'll still owe him forty-five dollars. He'll find a way to collect. It's the principle of the thing.

I give her the ring at the station. Just open the little box and let her see it, and she bursts out crying and buries her face in my coat and says things I can't make out.

She holds out her finger, and I slip the ring on, and from the look in her eyes I figure she was saying yes things.

I never actually ask the question, but by now there really is no question, that's just the point. If it was a matter of asking or not asking or what the question is, I wouldn't be in this situation. The situation, as I see it, is this: Are you a decent guy, or are you not? Time to choose up sides.

Then I'm broadsided by Andrew's mother. She gets my sleeves in a death grip and hugs and kisses me.

She says, "You be good boys, be good boys, both of you, and Walter—take care of Andrew. You'll take care of him, won't you?"

This is more words than I've ever heard Andrew's mother string together all at one time. Usually she's painfully shy. Calling her the silent type would be understating the case.

I don't say I will. I don't say I won't. I just stand there with what must be a really stupid look on my face, and then I shoot Andrew a wild-eyed look, and he comes and retrieves her.

Now my dad slaps me on the back, says we're off on the greatest adventure of our lives. A time we'll never forget. We'll feel alive. We'll feel like men. We'll know our purpose.

I really love my dad, but right at this moment I wish he would shut up. I wish I could tell him that's easy to say when you served in peacetime.

I look over his shoulder to my mom. I can tell she's not so sure. But she would never contradict him.

Then the conductor says all aboard, so we get on the train.

I look at Mary Ann through the window. My fiancée. I know I did the right thing. From everything I've ever been taught, I know it's right.

She moves her lips and says, I love you. I mouth the words back. But it's different the way she says it.

Then I look at my mom, and she's crying.

I look at my dad, and he swings his fist in this little jab that I take to mean, Go get 'em, boy. Go kill you some Japs for God and country.

I look to my kid brother and sister and notice they haven't said a word. You can't help wondering what somebody's thinking when they won't say. Poor Robbie. He doesn't really know how to say what he means. He's like me in that respect, only worse. Usually Katie says whatever comes into her head, only nobody takes it seriously. Nobody pays a damn bit of attention. So what's worse, if you're expected not to show your feelings, or if you're expected to show them so they can be disregarded?

Honestly, the choices we give a poor kid. No wonder we have wars.

Just as the train pulls out, I look to Andrew's mother, and it hits me.

Me take care of Andrew?

I thought Andrew was going to take care of me.

This war thing was all his idea, and besides, I'm the one who's already out of prayers.

CHAPTER SEVEN

Michael

He crumples his third letter to Mrs. Whittaker, makes a perfect three-point shot into the wastebasket. The other two letters lie against the baseboard.

He had no idea how hard this was going to be. It's the closest thing to homework he's had in years, and as inscrutable as calculus. His resentment mounts to a place he can actually feel. It's just underneath his ears.

He's tried saying he's an old friend of Walter's from the war, but it's a risk. Andrew might know all of Walter's army buddies.

Then he tried saying he's just a friend, no specifics. But the more questions they ask—Andrew and Mrs. Whittaker—the more he'll be on the spot. And if they insist on meeting him, he's dead. He's forty years too young.

In the third version he's an author writing a book about World War II, but he can't explain why Walter would come into it, with thousands of live veterans to interview.

It's no use.

He can't explain what he doesn't understand himself.

He feels cheated by Walter, whoever Walter is, this spirit, this movement on a Ouija board, because Walter promised that when he found Andrew, he would know what to do.

And it's not true.

Feeling he has a legitimate gripe, he roots around in Dennis's closet and finds the board. He settles with it on his lap, sets the pointer in place, touches his fingers lightly to it, and rattles off a string of complaints.

It feels strange to have grown so comfortable with this board and whatever speaks through it. It might be a sign that he has lost it. In the back of his mind, that possibility looms.

"Okay," he says in the general direction of the board. "I found him, and you were wrong. I have no idea what to do. He won't talk to me until I say why I need him to. I can't tell him the truth. What the hell am I supposed to do now? All I said I would do is find him."

Silence. No movement on the board. Maybe he shouldn't have yelled.

"I did what you wanted. I found him."

The pointer moves now. Slides to the word NO

"No? What do you mean, 'no'? His wife says he knows you. Are you saying I've got the wrong guy?"

NO

"Then I found him."

NO

Do Ouija boards stick? Frustrated, he picks up the envelope and waves it in front of the board, as if it has eyes, then feels embarrassment for the gesture.

"Okay, listen. Andrew F. Whittaker, 342 68th St. NW, Albuquerque, New Mexico. I found him."

The pointer spells out words for the first time this session. It spells out THATS HIS ADDRESS

"I know that's his address, damn it, what do you think I'm trying to tell you? I knew it was his address when I read it to you."

Dennis hears him shouting, pokes his head into the room, shoots him a funny, tilted look.

"Maybe if you weren't so antagonistic with the spirit world, man, it wouldn't be so hard on you."

Michael signals him to leave, then closes his eyes and tries to breathe smoothly. In that moment, as he quiets himself, he realizes what the words on the board are trying to say.

"Okay, I get it. You're saying I found his address, not him."

YES

"Oh, shit." It sweeps over him then, obvious and unavoidable. "You mean I actually have to go out there and find him? Like, in person?"

After a pause, the pointer spells methodically, ID APPRECIATE IT

Michael sighs. "At least you're a polite spirit. Look, I have to think about this. I've already been told that Andrew doesn't want to talk to me. So I go all that way and look him in the face. Then what?"

YOULL KNOW

"Perfect," he says. "That's just perfect."

He puts the board back in Dennis's closet.

· ★ ·

Michael buys a cheap street map of Albuquerque on his way into town. He's hot, tired, frustrated from stopping every fifty miles or so to refill his leaky radiator. He hasn't slept nearly enough. He can feel that scratchy fact, and is pretty sure it shows.

His van has no air-conditioning.

He has no idea why he's going to all this trouble.

He parks in front of the house, notes that it looks pretty much like any other on the street, wonders why he expected otherwise.

It's painted a burnt orange—very Southwest—a two-tone garage with the shape of a teepee on the door. Every aspect modest but neatly tended. Someone with patience lives here. Someone willing to not only mow, but manicure.

Michael has never fully understood people who concentrate on their environment.

He takes a deep breath, marches up the walk. Knocks.

He feels a wave of doubt that doubles as a dizzy spell. Shouldn't he have prepared a few words? My God, someone will come to the door now, and he has no idea what to say. Walter said he would know. Somehow, though, with footsteps on the other side of the door, that assurance isn't nearly enough.

Andrew opens the door.

In the flash of an instant before he does, Michael arrives at the first thing he should say. Hello. Are you Mr. Whittaker? It's simple, but it seems to fit the bill.

He doesn't say it.

Because when Andrew answers the door, he knows it's Andrew.

He can tell.

Oh, he looks different, he looks forty years older, but he's aged in all the ways one might expect. He still has that long, straight nose, that knack for critical appraisal. His eyes are still sharp and cutting but set a little too close together. He still stands with his shoulders back, almost too straight, like a joke about posture.

So his hair is white. He's still Andrew.

And since Michael has never met or seen Andrew before, this realization throws him off his rhythm, if he had one.

He stares.

Andrew says, "Yes? May I help you, young man?"

Michael wonders why Andrew doesn't know him, then wonders why he wondered that.

He looks into the room behind him, sees Mary Ann, and draws his breath in a gasp. The inside of his head tingles, as if his brain has fallen asleep. He feels he won't draw another breath unless he consciously forces the issue.

"Mary Ann? What the hell are you doing here?" It slips out of him before he can think it through.

Andrew turns, looks to his wife, then back to Michael. "You two know each other?"

But Mary Ann only stares back.

Andrew's voice rises. "Will someone please tell me what's going on here?"

Michael pulls his gaze off Mary Ann and looks Andrew square in the eye.

"This is your wife?" he asks.

"Yes. Now who the hell are you?"

"I can't believe you did it, Andrew. You married my girl."

"What?"

"I trusted you."

"Who are you?" Andrew bellows. "What are you talking about?"

It startles Michael, snaps him out of something he never understood he'd been in, and he wonders the same things himself. "I . . . my name is Michael Steeb. I . . . just forget what I said a minute ago. I have no idea what I was talking about."

He wants to go on to explain that it's unlike him to be irrational, but knows he'll only dig himself in deeper, whatever he says. Then he realizes he's found Andrew, in person, and his job is over. Thank God. Walter said that was all he needed to do, and damn it, Michael feels willing to take him at his word on that.

"I'll just be going now," he says.

As he burns rubber down 68th St. NW, in his rearview mirror he sees Andrew, standing on his manicured front lawn, watching him go.

· ★ ·

It's an eighteen-hour drive home, so he has plenty of time to think it over, but his brain seems ill-equipped for the job. If he tries to understand, it short-circuits immediately, like a kindergartner trying to learn quantum physics.

Instead, he lets his thoughts wander to a past he's sure he never had.

He remembers that Mary Ann's hair was red before it was gray, and he remembers the wrist corsage she wore to the prom. He remembers that she liked the lemon pie Walter's mom used to make, though nobody liked it as much as Walter did, and that she was the only girl who would actually let Nicky jump up and lick her face.

What about his own memories? he wonders as he drives. What about his own prom, which he ditched? What about his own high school girlfriend? Why does he miss Walter's more?

He can only assume that Walter's memories have tangled with his own somehow, which explains that humiliating incident at Andrew's door, but he's too mentally exhausted to care why, and he knows he can't figure out the answer anyway. He knows that understanding this situation, if such a thing is possible, has nothing to do with applied logic.

He decides to stop over one night and sleep in his van.

In his dream he sits by his own creek, playing saxophone, and Walter comes and sits quietly beside him.

He's a tall, broad-shouldered young man, about Michael's age. Dark. Dark hair, dark eyes, a heavy, dark beard grown out into five o'clock shadow.

He has a cleft in his chin, like Cary Grant. His uniform is torn in several places.

He looks like someone Michael knows. Someone he'd want to know, if he didn't already. Someone he'd meet on a bus or a stool at a lunch counter and just start right up talking to, because he'd be able to tell that Walter would be easy to know, and he wouldn't be sorry for the effort.

His eyes are so brown they're almost black. They've seen things, those eyes.

Michael stops playing the sax and shakes Walter's hand. His grip is warm and reassuring.

Michael says, "I messed it all up."

"No," Walter says, "you did fine."

"It was a mess. You said I'd know what to do."

"You did fine."

"You mean that's all I had to do?"

"Absolutely."

"So everything's fine now?"

"It will be."

Satisfied by his tone, Michael takes up his saxophone again and plays, mellow and sad.

Walter seems content to sit and listen. Then he lies down with his hands behind his head, looking up at the clouds.

The music sounds good, better than it ever has before.

CHAPTER EIGHT

Walter

It's not my intention to apologize for Andrew, and that's not what I'm about to do. But I want you to know a little of what he was like when I knew him.

Of course, in some ways, what he is now is what he was then. You just have to know him.

Like when I'm in the hospital. That's where I am. After that little incident with the mortar round. Okay, I'm confusing you, and I don't mean to. This doesn't have anything to do with getting my head blown off. This is a few weeks earlier in my run of bum luck. It's that time I don't like to talk about, but I'll skip the bad part.

He comes to see me the first day. Well, the first day I'm conscious, anyway.

I'm depressed. Because of what was happening when I got hit, but he doesn't know that yet and neither do you. Also because I'd gotten a look at my body that morning when they changed the dressing. First good look since it happened. My first real devastating injury.

It shakes you up.

You find out you've kind of grown attached to your body all smooth and right, the way it was supposed to be. Even though you never thought about it before.

The first thing I say when I see him is, "Andrew! My God. I thought you were dead."

It's like I'm seeing a ghost.

He says, "Aw, hell, nothing can kill me." Then nobody knows what to say.

It's funny, good friends as we are, how much of the time we don't know what the hell to say to each other. Then he thinks of something, but it's a bad something.

He says, "Did you at least get the guy?"

"What guy?"

"The guy you went out after."

See, this is a perfect example of how he is. I never told him I went out after a guy. He put it together that way because he likes it that way. He drew his own picture.

Me, I always did hate to burst his bubble.

So I say, "Well, I got two at the entrance, but then all I got was an ass-whipping."

He laughs and lets that be the end of it. "Well, two anyway. Good work."

I'm tempted to tell him to shut the hell up, but I don't.

See, this is the other reason for my depression, how before this whole thing came down I'd shot two Jap boys in the back. And it's funny how it won't sit with me, considering that's what we came over here to do.

It was the first time I'd ever actually killed somebody. And it wasn't supposed to matter because it was them, but I kept thinking, Don't Japanese mommas cry if their boys don't come home? It's one of those things you figure will be okay, and then it happens. Nobody really prepares you for when it happens. How can they? I guess.

I will never, never tell him that part. He wouldn't know what to do with it. He wouldn't hear it, because if he heard it, where would he put it?

Anyway, he doesn't want me to be depressed, so he puts himself in charge of cheering me up.

Starts bringing me stacks of mail from home. I begin to suspect he solicited their help.

My brother Robbie tells me all about his baseball team, how he hit a double. He never could hit before, no matter how hard we practiced. I love the kid like crazy, and I don't think any less of him for it, but he's not a born athlete. Maybe he got lucky. Maybe he's lying through his teeth.

My mom tells me all about other guys we know who went off to war, sons of people from Ocean City or thereabouts, and how they're all still okay and not getting hurt. Like this is some proof that we'll all share the same fate. Like bad things only happen to people who don't live in New Jersey. Only to people we don't know.

My dad writes seven pages about the hardware store. Can

you imagine? How can a hardware store be seven pages' worth of interesting to anybody? It sure never will be to me.

That's a whole other thing that I'd best not get started on right now. Believe me, I could digress.

Katie sends me a bunch of little stickers on a page. Draws hearts and stuff. Not too many words, but I'm amazed they got her to write at all. It's sort of cute if you're in the mood for it.

I'm not.

The letters are all real upbeat, like somebody told them to write that way. Every little thing at home can't be as good as all that.

After a while I can't bring myself to read them. I can't explain why not, but reading them only makes it worse.

So Andrew comes in every day after mail call, dumps the letters on my bed. I set them on the floor.

He says, "Come on. Aren't you even going to read them?"

I say, "Later, after you're gone."

I make it sound like I can't stand to miss a minute of his visit, and he buys that because he needs to buy it or it won't fit right in his brain.

That's a very good example of how he is.

Then, when the letters don't cheer me up, he brings me this magazine. To look at the cover, you'd think it was a back issue of *Stars and Stripes*. But that's only the cover. He's got a different sort of a magazine altogether stapled inside.

So I look through it, kind of let my eyes go wide, because I know that reaction will make him happy.

Somebody tells me by and by that he traded a whole carton of cigarettes for that thing. A little pricey if you ask me.

I stick it under my pillow.

Sex drive is a funny thing with me anyway, and I've just been blown into little fragments and sewn back together wrong. Not that there was really much damage to my privates. It's more what it did on the inside that's holding me back.

Now, of course, I have to be careful with the damn magazine, because if any of the hospital staff get a look at it, they'll want another look, and then I'll never see it again. I should just let them take it, but I feel responsible to Andrew, because it's a well-meant gift.

So I keep it under my pillow, and when they come to change the bed, I pass it over to Billy Ray, the Texan boy next door, and he puts it under his pillow. Then when they get to him, he slips it back.

In return, I let him use it on alternate nights, so at least somebody gets some good out of it.

The upshot of all this deception is that I let Andrew think things are picking up with me. Actually, what I'm doing is letting go of life, of caring. That seems to represent an upswing, at least from the outside. Funny how that goes.

And Andrew, he needs to fix things. He needs for things to be okay, and if they get out of kilter, he needs to fix them. So I let him think he fixed me.

I wonder sometimes why I do all this for him.

No, I don't, really. I know. It's because I love him. What I wonder, really, is why I don't do as much for me.

I'm not trying to sell you on Andrew. I'm not trying to say all that cheering-up garbage in the hospital was selfless, or a great favor to me, or even a good thing. It was misguided.

But I don't blame him for it, either.

It's just whistling in the graveyard, is what it is.

He did a lot of that during the war, and I hope he hasn't lost the tune. Because, poor Andrew, he has no idea what's about to hit him. I mean, on the one hand it's almost funny. From the big perspective of out here you could have a good laugh. But for a guy like Andrew, this is a tough thing coming at him. I really feel kind of sorry for him.

He's a big jerk, but he's also my best friend.

He'll be in a new territory now, with nowhere to stand and nothing to fight.

If anything, he's going to have to whistle louder in his old age.

CHAPTER NINE

Michael

Michael wakes in the morning, smokes a joint before getting out of bed. It's warm in the house, and he walks to the sink in only boxer shorts and begins to brush his teeth.

He hears a car out front, its wheels crunching on the gravel, figures it's Dennis leaving, wants to catch him before he goes into town. There are several items on a shopping list that Dennis was likely—characteristically—too busy to check before leaving.

Michael trots down the unfinished, unrailed stairs, throws the front door open, ready to run out across the porch. He stops on a dime to keep from smacking into Mary Ann.

She stands poised to knock. She wears a blue cotton suit and nylons, her silvery hair all in place, fresh out of the beauty parlor. It's a look out of synch with the land, the old tractor, the automobile junkyard. The house they'll finish building someday.

In her eyes he finds a strange combination of terror and hope. He wonders briefly if he might have looked the same, standing on their doorstep in Albuquerque, hoping no one would call upon him to say why. Now it's his turn not to ask.

He swallows, forgetting his mouth is full of toothpaste, tries to talk, but it's garbled. He takes two steps backwards and waves her in. Then he bolts upstairs and pulls on a pair of jeans.

He comes down with his mouth rinsed, feeling apologetic though he's not sure why. His heart pounds in his chest, no matter how he shushes and berates it.

Mary Ann says, "Hello, Mr. Steeb. I'm sorry I caught you at a bad moment."

"Michael."

"Michael."

They stare at each other in silence, and he feels as though some part of him withers and dies in his inability to function.

"I know there's something I want to say to you, Mary Ann. Except I'll be damned if I know what it is."

She tries to smile, but it's hard for her, he can tell.

"I know you're interested in Walter," she says, "so I brought some things you might like to look at. I'm thinking they might mean something to you."

"You came all this way to see me," he says, forgetting

to wonder what the things are. He hears himself talking to her like a sweetheart, and it feels fitting, as if there's really no other voice he could use. "You didn't tell Andrew, did you?"

"Oh, no. I couldn't very well do that. He was very upset by your visit. I told him I was going to see my sister in San Francisco. I'll have to do that before I go back, so as not to make a liar out of myself."

She opens her bag and pulls out a framed portrait of Walter in his dress uniform. Michael recognizes him immediately as the young man who sat on the creek bank in his dream, his presence seeming to make Michael's sax sound better somehow.

The frame is silver, maybe real silver, and not the least bit tarnished, either. Michael has never owned much silver, but he guesses you'd have to polish a frame like that every few days to keep it in such good shape. It speaks to something, and Michael feels himself straining to hear more.

He draws a deep breath, but it doesn't seem to want to blow out again, and he has to push.

He says, "This is real, isn't it?" His voice shakes.

She doesn't answer.

He takes the frame out of her hands, and his eyes stop on the ring. She wears it on her right hand. It looks so old-fashioned now, in its heavy white-gold setting. He grasps her hand in his and stares at it.

He hears himself say, in that sweetheart voice, "I thought you'd take that off and put it in a drawer."

"Thank you," she says. "Now I know I didn't drive all this way for nothing. And also, never. I would never take it off."

He feels awkward, suddenly unbalanced, standing close to her, half naked, holding her hand. He lets go and steps back. But her eyes seem to close the distance again.

"I'm sorry I can't offer you much," he says. "There's no electric yet. This is kind of like camping. We could go into town and have breakfast. I'm sorry."

"Please don't be."

"Why did you marry him?"

Michael is stunned to hear himself say it. And yet as it comes out he feels the pressure that sent it. It's a sudden retroactive change of history. As if he looked up and saw an unfamiliar chair in his house and at the same time knew it had been there for years. Except a chair would have been more welcome.

She opens her mouth to speak, but he cuts her off. "No, that's a stupid question. Don't even answer it. Walter was dead. Why shouldn't you have married him? I'm sorry."

He turns to the kitchen, like he's going to get something, but there's nothing to get. He just needs to use himself, to get away. He suddenly can't stand still.

Mary Ann has not managed to reply.

"It just pisses me off. Pardon my language."

"I know. I can tell."

"So what else did you bring to show me? You said you brought something else."

He motions her over to a mattress that serves as a sofa, and she sits down, tucking her skirt carefully around her. He feels a pang of guilt for asking her to sit there. It's not clean enough. Nothing here is. It's not good enough for her. He should have more to offer her than this.

She pulls out another photo, this one small and dog-eared, and sets it on his open hand.

"Oh, God. The four musketeers."

Walter, Andrew, Bobby, and Jay. The first day they landed on that stinking island. It brings back more than he cares to remember. He sets it on the mattress between them. Maybe later he will look at that photo for hours, but just now he needs to set it aside.

"I have no idea what all this means, Mary Ann. Do you?"

He allows himself to bring his eyes up to hers. He knows she's been studying him.

"Do I know? Or could I explain?"

The silence falls again.

She reaches into her bag, this time pulls out a small, flat box. He feels himself recoil inside. He doesn't know what it is, but he feels he doesn't want to touch it. She sets it on his lap, and he opens it gingerly, as if it might contain a rattlesnake. Inside is something much worse. An army medal.

"Walter's Purple Heart," Mary Ann says.

She didn't need to say that. He knows what it is. He snaps the box shut and hands it back. He wonders if his face is pale. It feels bloodless.

"I can't handle looking at that."

"Why not?"

"I didn't earn it. I mean—"

"Did you hear what you just said, Michael?"

"No, no, I never listen when I talk."

She smiles, maybe at his nervousness, maybe at her own.

She asks him if he believed in reincarnation before all this happened.

"Reincarnation? No. I mean, I never really think about it. I figure I'll worry about that stuff when I'm dead. Why? Is that what you think this is about?"

"Can you explain it some other way?"

"Well, I just thought I had this guy, this spirit, who kind of latched on to me. I used to talk to him on the Ouija board."

"But his past is familiar to you."

"Yeah, I don't get that part, either."

In a sudden decision, he stands and runs upstairs, taking two steps at a time. He finds the Ouija board, stops to put on a shirt, thinking it'll make him feel more secure.

As he carries the board downstairs, he thinks of the first thing Walter said to him. *Don't be afraid. It's only you.*

He sits down beside her and sets the board on his lap. Breathes deeply. If this is about reincarnation—which he may or may not even believe in—then he has been talking to himself. Which is really the only development that could make this whole situation any more bizarre.

"How do you do this," she says. "Do you ask it something?"

Before he can even answer, the pointer all but takes off without him.

It spells out HI MARY ANN

Mary Ann's eyes moisten, and her face looks tight, anguished. It's hard to tell if this is a good moment or a bad one.

Michael asks, "Is this a reincarnation thing? Is that the part I don't get?" But asks who? That's a question still floating, without forming into real words, at the back of his mind.

The pointer slides to the word YES

"I used to be you?"

YES

He doesn't dare look at Mary Ann's reaction.

"I'm still really confused. How come you're so . . . you. I mean, if you got born again, and you're me now, why are you so separate? Why can't you just be Michael?" Wasn't that the way it was supposed to work?

He waits an unusually long time for the answer, then it's spelled out slowly.

I WASNT DONE BEING WALTER. I THINK IM STUCK

Mary Ann lets slip an audible sob, and Michael lends her his handkerchief.

· ★ ·

They sit on opposite sides of a table in the only decent restaurant in town. The walls are decorated with old fruit-crate labels, shellacked onto the dark paneling. More fruit-crate labels cover the table between them, a thick, clear layer bonding them down like liquid glass.

Michael watches Mary Ann's hands, noticing the strange combination of familiar and unfamiliar. He could do the same with her face, but if he did, she'd return his stare. Meet his eyes. Embarrass him. With his eyes slightly averted from her face, much of this feels okay, feels possible. Like something he can really do. Out the window, Michael watches a smattering of locals cruising through the parking lot in their mostly rusty pickups. Another juxtaposition of familiar and not.

He says, "Nothing fancy, but the food is decent here. They make great French toast."

"I love French toast."

"I know. That's why I brought it up."

That knocks them back into a silence that lasts until after the waitress has come for their order.

Now Michael has spent an hour or two in her presence, and his head is filled to overflowing with childhood memories. Except the childhood is not his own. He feels it bubbling up, wanting to be talked about. He wants to reminisce.

"Remember when I used to walk you home from school?" he asks. He has more to say, but her eyes come up to meet his, and the words freeze in his throat. He pushes himself to continue. "You said you needed the protection. Because of—"

"That dog."

"Right. That big red dog. I could never figure out why they didn't just keep that monster in the yard. He was so mean."

"Not to you, he wasn't. You faced him right down. I never saw anything so brave."

Michael laughs. Brave, right. That's me. Walter. Me. "I practically wet my pants every time."

"No you didn't."

"You have no idea."

"But you looked him right in the eye and stamped at him and said, 'Go home!' and he did."

"What was I supposed to do, let him eat you?"

He hears it slip into his voice again, that sweet something. That dating voice. His heart feels bigger and fuller when he looks at her. Every time she glances away, he looks at her face to feel his heart get bigger. Nothing has made his heart feel this big, not for so long. But if Mary Ann is the cause of it, then whose heart is in question here? And are there two to choose from? It all feels very much beyond his grasp.

"Remember?" she says. "We ran into those people one night. On the beach."

"What people?"

"With the dog. I mean, they weren't with the dog. But we knew it was their dog. You asked them straight out, why didn't they keep that dog in the yard. Remember?"

Michael furrows his brow for a moment. He wants to remember, but he doesn't. He shakes his head. "No. What did they say?"

"They said, 'Elmo? Elmo is so sweet.' Well, maybe it wasn't Elmo, maybe it was Arnold or something. You don't remember that. Okay. Then later we were walking on the beach and it was dark and it seemed like we were completely alone, so you kissed me. I remember because it was only the third time you kissed me. And it turned out your kid brother had followed us down there and was watching from behind one of the pier pilings."

Robbie. Michael remembers Robbie. It hurts and feels good to think his name, all in the same complicated sensation. "He didn't mean anything by it."

"I know. I didn't mean—"

"He was a good kid. People didn't always understand him."

"I didn't mean—"

"He sort of lived his life through me. You know what I mean?"

They hold each other's eyes for a moment.

"I think so," she says.

Michael desperately wants to ask a simple question. How is Robbie? Where is Robbie? Is there still a Robbie? Who is he now? Did he get stuck with the hardware store? But he can't bring himself to spit out the words. What if he wouldn't like the answer? He feels that bad news about Robbie would be almost more than he could take.

Then he feels guilty and disloyal because he has a real brother of his own, a brother from this life, Roger, and he never calls Roger. And although he certainly wouldn't care to hear bad news about Roger, he doesn't feel as though his life would stop if he did.

It makes his insides feel thick and painful, suddenly having two difficult pasts to sort out.

The waitress brings their French toast. She hovers slightly before moving off.

"Mike," she says. "Aren't you going to introduce me? I just know this has to be your grandmother, because we already met your mom."

Michael introduces her simply as Mary Ann.

When the waitress leaves, he says, "I'm really sorry."

"It's not your fault."

"I know. I'm just really sorry."

CHAPTER TEN

Walter

I should've paid more attention to my little brother. I knew that at the time, and I know it now. He needed me. Only problem was, I needed me, too.

This family thing. It's like you're all thrown together, trying to get by somehow, and there's not enough of something. It's really hard to put my finger on what that something is, but believe me, there's not enough. So here's my poor kid brother begging me for some of mine, but I'm nearly starving as it is. And the weird part is, we can't even say what it is we're missing. It's like you can feel the hole, but you don't know what's supposed to fill it, because it's something you've never seen.

You don't want it to be every man for himself, but it sort of is. And there's not much you can do about it.

I don't mean to talk in riddles.

The worst memory I have of that poor kid is the day I tell my mom I'm not taking the store. Robbie walks into the kitchen and overhears us. I don't even know he's there at first. He has a way of doing that. I swear the kid is invisible in some very real way.

I'm telling my mom that when I get back from the war, I'm going to California. I won't even say why yet, for what, because I know it sounds so stupid.

She's filling the salt and pepper shakers, and she won't even look up at me. Not at first. Then she looks up, but she doesn't even say it. Just looks at me, and we both know the words, so I have to speak them. She doesn't even have to say it, but I have to answer. I have to defend myself. Family law.

"He'll get over it," I say, but it's a lie. He won't. Not my dad. He'll die still not over it.

That's when I look up and see Robbie standing in the kitchen doorway. I'll never forget the look on his face. It's my worst memory of him. It's the thing I'd most like to change if I could.

I try to say something to him, but he runs outside. I go out and try to find him. I look in the garage, in the tree house. I look in the yard, in the neighbors' yards. I walk into town and look for him in the library, the soda shop, the arcade. I know I have to find him and say something to him, so I'm trying to find him even though I have no idea what to say.

Finally I give up and go home.

There's Robbie, in my bedroom, lying on my bed, looking

up at my ceiling. I have astronomy maps on my ceiling. Con-
stellations. You could look at that stuff for a long time.

"Then *I'll* have to," he says.

I sit on the edge of the bed with him. He has fierce eyes,
Robbie. Everywhere he goes he walks like he's late for a fight.

"You don't have to do anything."

"Crowley and Sons Hardware," he says. "He's got the
sign, Walter. He already made the sign. He can paint out the
letter *S*, I guess, but I'll still have to do hardware."

"He can paint out everything but Crowley Hardware."

"No, he can't," Robbie says. "It'd leave too much space.
You have to do it with me, Walter."

"I can't."

I have these plans. For my life. I want to *be* something. I'm
sure Robbie does, too. But he'll just have to learn to say no in
his own time, in his own way. It'll be hard, believe me, I know.
But it's not something I can do for him. I'll always feel guilty,
though, because the second "no" is ten times harder, and we
both know it. Our dad only has two sons.

"Please," he says.

"I can't."

"What's so important?"

I can't really bring myself to say cartoons, so I say, "Life."

"Don't decide till after the war, okay? Maybe the war'll
change things."

"It won't."

"Promise me you won't decide till you come home."

"*If* I come home," I say.

That's the wrong thing to say. He stomps out of my room

and out of the house and down the street. He doesn't come back until after dark, and he doesn't speak to me for three days.

I leave a note on his pillow that says, "I'll wait and decide after the war."

He still doesn't speak to me. But he leaves a note on my pillow.

It says, "Don't *ever* say that again."

And I don't think he means the part about ditching the store and moving to California. In fact, I know he doesn't. He means the *If*. The *If* was a mistake. One of those words that should only have happened in my head.

So we leave it that way. That I'll wait to decide. Even though I know I've decided. Postponing the inevitable. But the least I can do is wait. He asked me nicely to wait. He thinks the war will change something.

And, of course, it will.

I have a sister, too. Katie. I don't talk about her as much. It's not that I don't notice her. I do. I try to be nice.

She needs something, too.

The difference is, Robbie asks me straight out. Begs me. Katie wouldn't take anything from me if I gift-wrapped it. She's set up for loss. That's what I think, anyway. She's built herself around that big hole, and she's attached to what she's built.

She doesn't want anybody messing up the balance of things by doing something stupid like loving her.

Sometimes I give her a little pat on the shoulder, or I'll put my arm around her if I see her on the street.

She shakes me off like I'm poison.

"Goon," she says, walking away as fast as she can. "Loser."

I love my brother, Robbie, but not enough to save him. I love my sister, Katie, but I've learned to do it from a distance.

This is how we grow. Have you noticed that? This is what we call loving each other.

No wonder we have wars.

CHAPTER ELEVEN

Mary Ann

In her sixth hour at Michael's house, her world is new. She sits in the dirt, her back against a tree, wiggles her bare feet in the grass. She looks down at the bright polish on her toenails, the only thing left that looks out of place.

She wears a pair of jeans borrowed from Michael's roommate. Michael's would have been too small in the hips. His big, dark sweatshirt engulfs her in a comfortable way. She pushes the bunchy sleeves up above her elbows.

Michael says, "You can cry if you need to. Don't stop on my account."

"No, it's just silly. I've had forty years to cry."

Michael is dismantling a motorcycle. He has the cases off. She knows because he explains as he goes along. Now he's replacing the bearings.

"What sort of bearings?" she wants to know.

"Bottom ones," he says. "Bottom end."

He stops periodically to wipe grease onto an already greasy towel. She wants to take it out of his hand and wipe the smudge off his face. She doesn't.

She watches him under the most ideal circumstances, while he is preoccupied, not watching back.

It's only the eyes that would have tipped her off. That and a trace of body language that slips in and out like a shadow. She knows that in a minute, or a day, or a month, the impact of all this will catch her. She doesn't care to rush.

Meanwhile they have fallen into this new routine in a strange way, talking as if this were Walter and always had been, as though nothing much had changed, as if no time had gone by. So easy to do. So easy to snap out of later, and wonder.

Right at this moment the sun is out, the air is clear and cool and a little salty in a way it could never be in New Mexico, and she feels happy. Furthermore, she feels she has a right to the feeling and has no intention of chasing it away.

"Ever smoke pot?" he says. She doesn't answer right away. "If you had, you'd remember."

"No, in my day only musicians used that."

"I'm a musician."

"Well, that explains a lot, then."

"It's just, I really like having you here, and I want you to stay as long as you can, but, like . . . I just pretty much smoke the stuff all day long. It's me, you know?"

"Well, don't let me stop you."

"You sure? You wouldn't be offended?"

She breathes deeply before answering. She says, "It's a different world today than it was yesterday. Anything can happen today."

"Thanks," he says, and pulls a rolled joint from his shirt pocket. He lights it, pulls deeply, then gestures in her direction. An offer.

She takes it.

"Your mind is very free," he says. "I like that about you."

"Thank you. How do you do this?"

"Just inhale, and don't exhale until you have to. Keep your lips open a little, so you get lots of air with it. Otherwise you'll cough it out."

She inhales, her throat seizes, but she swallows hard, postponing the inevitable for a few precious seconds. Her lungs are full of a gift, of sorts, from her host, and it doesn't seem right to waste it.

She hands it back, coughing. Michael asks if she wants a glass of water. She says no, she's fine. She reaches for the joint again, and he hands it to her. She tries to hold it by the part that isn't greasy.

The next time she reaches for it, he holds back. "Ride with that a while."

"Excuse me?"

"Wait a few minutes. It kinda sneaks up on you."

Mary Ann leans her head back against the trunk of the

tree, looks up to the clouds through the shifting leaves. She invites it to sneak up on her, and it does.

It makes the top of her head tingle in a warm sort of way, it drops her into a sense of well-being that she knows is drug induced, but which feels natural, as if the universe had always been this perfect if she had only once stopped to notice.

Faintly, as if far away, she hears him explain that some people get "real high" the first time, while others feel nothing at all.

She tilts her head back down and smiles at him. She wonders if it's the same way she used to smile. She can't tell.

"Case number one," he says.

"Michael. I'm going to tell you now—why I married him."

"You don't have to do that."

"Hush now and listen. For a few months everybody was very patient with me. They said, 'We understand, dear, you've suffered a terrible loss.' Then they started to push. They said I wasn't getting on with my life. I knew that. Why would I want to?"

She listens with interest to her own words. They sound competent, effortless. They make the complexity of her emotion sound as if it has been childishly simple all these years. So easy to explain. It surprises her.

"They said take off that ring and put it away, otherwise no boy will ever ask you out. Then Andrew got sent home with that injury, and Walter's mother fixed us up and we went out and talked about you all night. I couldn't have done that with any other man. How many men would let me wear this engagement ring on my right hand for forty years? Or keep Walter's picture on my desk all this time?"

Michael sits with his legs apart, taps his wrench lightly on the dirt. "Did you ever tell him?"

"Tell him what?"

"You know."

There's something weighty in the way he says it. In the way he suddenly holds his wrench.

"Do I?" She doesn't think she does.

"Does he know you weren't a virgin when you married him?"

She tries to consider that a moment, but it's hard. She's never before had to consider anything while stoned. It never occurred to her that Andrew didn't know.

"I just assumed Walter had told him. They told each other everything."

"Then he doesn't know."

"Oh, dear God. I just assumed he knew."

"I didn't tell him."

She rolls this over a bit, tries to see everything through the new perspective, then forgets what she's supposed to be thinking about.

"Oh." She drops her head back again and looks up through the trees. "Think you'll finish fixing it today?"

"I'll be lucky if I finish this month. I have to rebuild the whole bottom end."

"Too bad. I never rode on a motorcycle before."

"You want a ride on a bike, just say so. I got lots of bikes. They don't look too pretty, but one of 'em runs."

· ★ ·

He finds her a pair of boots, and the four pairs of socks it will take to keep them on her feet.

She wishes for a mirror but can't find one. She wants to see how much she has changed since the sun came up. Wants to see the new Mary Ann with her own eyes, having a sense she will like her.

She climbs on to the beat-up dirt bike behind Michael, wraps her arms loosely, a bit awkwardly, around his narrow waist.

He kicks the starter, and the motor jumps to life.

"No muffler!" he yells, though it's obvious. "You're going to have to hold on tighter than that. This thing bites."

She squeezes him tightly, and the bike stutters, jumps, and takes off.

The revving of the engine blocks out all other sounds; the wind brings tears to her eyes and whips hair into her face, some of it Michael's, some her own. It doesn't matter that her hair is messy. Not anymore.

He winds uphill, cutting around curves, the bike leaning nervously close to the ground, a plume of brown dirt kicked up in its wake.

She thinks she can feel the changes in the temperature, in the density of the air as they climb. The rhythm of vibration comes up through the seat to meet her, changing with the terrain and the shifting of gears.

"You okay?" he yells.

"I like it."

At the top of the hill, he spins to a stop and cuts the throttle to a quieter idle.

She looks down across the house, the orchards; the neighboring hills, their houses, their orchards. The abandoned cars and tractors, rusty house trailers, grazing horses, black-and-white cows.

"I can see the ocean from here. I've been in Albuquerque too long. It's so flat there."

"Did you always live in Albuquerque?"

"Don't you remember?"

He doesn't answer at first. Then he says, "Don't tell me. I'll think awhile. I'll get it." He walks the bike backwards and heads it down the hill. "Someplace with a boardwalk, right?"

Then he hits the throttle again.

· ★ ·

"I want a picture of you," she says. She pulls an automatic camera out of her bag. She stands him out on the porch, in front of the house-in-progress.

"Shouldn't I even clean up or something?"

"No, just like that."

She wants the grease, the brown dirt, the sweat. Everything that belongs in the picture.

Just as she snaps the shutter, Dennis drives up. This roommate she keeps hearing about. He walks up onto the porch hesitantly, as though he's accidentally arrived at the wrong half-built house.

"Hey, Mary Ann, this is my roommate, Dennis. Dennis, Mary Ann. This is Andrew's wife."

"Oh," Dennis says. "I see." But he looks like he doesn't.

"Hey, Dennis, take a picture of me and my girl, okay?"

She tries to argue, but he grabs her around the waist and pulls her to his side.

"My hair, though."

"I got it. It's covered." He pulls a plastic comb out of his back pocket and combs her hair straight back along her head. "Much better. Now you look like a motorcycle momma."

Dennis tells them to smile. They're already smiling.

CHAPTER TWELVE

Michael

He lies on his back on the cool wooden floorboards, shirt open, hands behind his head. In the flickery light of the candle, he can just see her face. She lies on her side on the makeshift couch, propped up on one elbow, staring down at him.

"Know what I think?" he says. "I think it was on the East Coast. Because I remember Andrew and I went down to the boardwalk once and watched the sun come up. And I think it was pretty close to Atlantic City, because Andrew and I borrowed my dad's car a couple of times to drive down there. But I can't come up with the name of the place. It's like I can get smells and sounds and visuals, but names are harder. When I try to remember, I blow a fuse. It's almost better if I don't think about it."

"Ocean City," she says. "It was Ocean City."

"How long can you stay?"

She sighs. "I told Andrew I'd be gone eight days, at the most. But it's a two-day drive, each way. And I have to go see my sister."

"You can't drive up to San Francisco tonight. You're too loaded."

"I know."

"Here. Have some more wine."

He sits up and pours the last of the bottle into her water tumbler.

She sips it thoughtfully.

"Can we smoke some more?" she asks.

He points to a carved wooden box, about the size of an old-fashioned cigarette box, and she opens it and pulls out a joint. She lights it and passes it to him.

"I like the feeling I get from it," she says on the exhale. "It keeps all this from seeming real. No. It makes it seem *more* real. It keeps *me* from seeming real, that's what it does."

He draws, exhales, passes it back to her. Says, "Huh?"

"Do you realize last night at this time none of this had happened yet? Do you see how much has changed?"

He tries to answer, but a fuse melts in his brain.

He lies still until he can think again.

Then he says, "How you gonna go back to him now? That's what I want to know."

She doesn't answer, and he decides not to look at her face.

The silence radiates, bounces off the walls and back into his ears. He thinks it's going to last forever, so he breaks it.

He says, "I'll get you a pillow and blanket." It feels good to get up and move around. Interfere with that moment that just squeezed him so hard. "Sorry," he says as he hands her the bedding. "It's not the Ritz."

She sets it down on the mattress behind her and moves in for a hug.

He freezes up for a split second, then hugs her back.

She feels warm in his arms, more than just her body temperature. Soft. Exaggeratedly real. He's too aware of the placement of his hands on her back.

He feels her breathing and thinks maybe he could stop and let her breathe for both of them. What a relief that would be. Maybe all he's ever wanted was to let go and float downstream. Find himself in his life some way other than alone.

Then he pulls away.

He says, "I'm going to need to talk to Andrew."

"Why?"

"For Walter's sake. It was his idea. He asked me to find Andrew. I think it's important."

"You did find him."

"It couldn't be enough."

"Leave it alone," she says. "Everything is changing. You couldn't stop it if you tried."

· ★ ·

Dennis is in the kitchen, sitting at the rough wooden table. Well, actually rough hardly says it. It's a huge old oak door resting on four empty cable spools. It's not high enough to get your knees under. He looks up as Michael comes through.

"Come," he says. "Sit."

Michael obeys like a good dog. He won't sleep if he goes to bed now, anyway.

Dennis has a glass of apple juice on the table in front of him, and he's making himself a bread-and-butter sandwich. "What gives?" he asks.

"Meaning what?"

Dennis gestures in the direction of the living room. "What exactly is the deal with her?"

"I told you. She's Andrew's wife."

"That's not what I mean. I mean how come you're mooning around here, acting like old sweethearts?"

Michael takes a deep breath. He was only half aware that they were. The half that knew and the half that didn't know collide now, forming one reality.

Through the kitchen window, in the moonlight, Michael can see five young deer crossing the kiwi orchard on their way down to the creek.

"Well, she's Walter's old sweetheart."

"I thought she was Andrew's wife."

"She was Walter's girl first." He points as he says it. He didn't expect the statement to come out with such vehemence, but it does.

Dennis raises his hands in a gesture of surrender. "Fine. Okay. Excuse me for asking a simple question. So somehow you're all moony over her because Walter was?"

Michael has no idea how to answer the question. First of all, he isn't entirely sure that Walter was. He has searched and searched for memories of Walter loving the hell out of that woman in his living room, but he keeps coming up blank. It's as if he's stumbled on the one part of the past that Walter isn't about to give up.

"Give me a break, Dennis," he says. "This is not the easiest thing in the world to explain."

· ★ ·

He sits out on the unrailed balcony, feet dangling into nothing, and lets the music live for itself. It sounds good tonight, feels good. It sounds like it feels. He records every note in a deep place in himself. Between the notes he hears the creek, crickets, wind in the leaves.

He hears her come out onto the porch underneath him. At first he thinks maybe he's making too much noise. But that's not it, and he knows it. She's not trying to sleep any more than he is. She heard the music, and it drew her outside.

He wonders if she's the one making the music feel so good.

He wonders if he should think about what's happening, pull it apart and ask it questions, but the wind and the moon say no. Who is he to overpower them?

Besides, he feels as if her presence on his farm, in his day, is a delicate thing, one that might disappear if he looks too closely. If he asks one question too many.

In time he sees her out of the corner of his eye. She's walked down the path to the creek, and she's sitting on the bridge, dangling her feet over the edge.

He can't see her face, but he can tell by the angle of her head that she's looking up at him.

He wonders if she can see that he's looking down at her.

She's wearing a white nightgown, and the breeze fills it, catches it, tosses it around her legs. It takes him a moment to notice that he has stopped playing to watch.

She looks like a ghost to him. He thinks maybe he looks like a ghost to her, too.

Then he thinks, Maybe that's all we are.

Maybe that's all we ever were.

CHAPTER THIRTEEN

Walter

Long before I got stuck like I am now, something was wrong with me. In what I liked, in what I thought was important.

Like, the whole time we were overseas, all I could talk about was getting home to a big piece of my mom's lemon pie. It drove Andrew batty after a while.

He'd yell at me.

He'd say, "Damn it, Walter, you've got a beautiful girl at home, and all you can think about is pie."

Once he broke down and admitted that he figured I'd gotten the pie mixed up with home, which may or may not be true. More often, he'd fly off the handle at anything that made it sound like I didn't appreciate what I had in that girl.

But I don't want to get into that habit of only thinking back on the bad times you had with somebody.

Those were bad times, I have to say, and Andrew and I had our share. Maybe more than our share. Sometimes when things happen you just let them go, one by one, because it's easier. You pretend they don't mean as much as they do. I should've had my eyes open about that, but you can't go back and second-guess things.

It's just that when we sat around and thought about the things we really loved, which you do when you're away at war, mostly what came to me were experiences. Not so much people. It seems I never tied my love up so much in any one person. It drove Andrew crazy, but what was I to do?

When I think back on the things I want to remember, it's all things he'd never understand. I think about sitting on the boardwalk in those white ducks, pulling bits of stale bread out of a paper sack to throw to the gulls.

That's where I am now.

They circle around over my head, calling to me. I throw the pieces of bread, and the birds dip down and catch them in midair. I like the sound they make, because they don't make it for just anybody. I like to think it's how you say my name in Seagull.

Or I think of the time I'm headed down to my dad's hardware store to work, and the guys from up the street come by in a pickup, ask if I want a ride. I jump in the back. It's hot summer, it's only seven in the morning, but you can feel the heat gearing to go. The breeze on my face feels good, like it's a lifesaver just to feel air move.

I got a pack of Lucky greens rolled into my shirtsleeve, so I pull out a smoke. Shield the flame with both hands and my knees. Then I lean back, way out over the edge of the truck bed, hands behind my head, and look up at the blue sky. Out of the corner of my eye, I see the wind burn my Lucky all down one side.

For reasons I can't explain, I feel alive, like the world's right here, I can see it, feel it, smell it. The sky looks so big, bigger than it ever did before. I'm welcome here if I want to be.

See, I'd never tell a thing like that to Andrew. He'd go crazy, say, "If I had the love of a girl like that, that's all I'd want to remember. That's all I'd care to know."

Lucky thing for him that I died.

He's right, though. She should have been what I fell back on, like when you hit that big empty place, when you need something to break your fall.

Like after Bobby died.

I really didn't tell you too much about that. Just that I threw up. But then there's that worse moment, when you stop throwing up and Bobby's still dead and somehow the show has to keep going and it's your job to make sure that it does.

I'm sorry to say it, but that's where I am.

I lie here in camp, awake all night, even though I'm tired enough to die on my feet. It rains again. This is an island known to take ten inches of rain in a single day. I'm not making that up. They recorded that one day when the 1st Marine

Division was here. Said the jeeps at Henderson Field sank in the mud up to their headlights, and it took three days to dig them out again.

We're trying to sleep in a sea of mud just about like that.

The mosquitoes bite me through the nets all night, and we all know the mosquitoes carry malaria.

And every time I close my eyes, I see Bobby's face. Wonder if tomorrow it'll be me or Andrew, staring up at nothing like that.

Andrew's right beside me, but what good does that do if I can't tell him I'm lost?

At a time like this, wouldn't you think a young soldier's thoughts would turn to his girl?

And all I can think about is sitting down in my mom's kitchen in the afternoon, smelling that pie just out of the oven. I think of Mom's hair, the way it tucks around her face in those soft waves, and her big skirts I used to hide behind when I was three and the iceman came. I think about her cutting me a big piece of pie and asking me how I did in track today. Or do we have a wrestling match coming up? Or do Andrew and I have plans for the evening?

Sometimes I think about real Lucky greens, not this crap they give us, and Coke in those nickel bottles that fit your hand just right.

And Nicky, my little mongrel dog, the way he'll wag his whole body when I come home.

If I come home.

Sometimes I think about Mary Ann. Mostly how she deserves better. How someone like her could take all that love and give it to a fool like me.

I think I don't know how to appreciate things. I want to. I can do it, only just in my head.

Like my dad, working hard all his life to build that business, so when I come home, I got some security. Some future. Crowley and Sons Hardware.

If I come home.

Do I appreciate it? Of course not. I want to move to Hollywood and try to get a job making cartoons. Is that the stupidest thing in the world for a guy to want to do?

I ask you, what's wrong with a guy like that?

But if I don't know, why do I think you will?

I have a confession to make. I interfered. Mixed into all this.

I went to see Andrew while she was gone.

Of course, he'll just think he had one of those funny realistic dreams.

In a way, Mary Ann was right when she said leave it alone. Everything's changing on its own.

But I'm the one with the most to lose here, and we'd hit a point where we could tip either way. It's like a snowball rolling downhill. If you're not careful, it might hit a flat spot, and then somebody'll have to give it a push. And who would that somebody be if not me?

I sat with him on the couch while he was napping. And I said, "Andrew, it's about your wife. She's not at her sister's."

Know what he said?

"Are you going to hurt me?"

Do you believe that? Am I going to hurt him. The person I love most in the world.

When he wakes up it'll start to eat at him.

Because Mary Ann almost never goes to her sister's that she doesn't pester him to go along. He knows that, but until he wakes up from this dream he won't think too much about it.

Then what she said will be true. Everything will change, and no one will be able to stop it.

I'm not trying to be a troublemaker. I'm really not. I'm just trying to get things done here. Sometimes things have to get a lot worse first, before they work out.

CHAPTER FOURTEEN

Michael

Late the following afternoon they return from town, where they had lunch and Mary Ann bought a pair of comfortable shoes.

While she changes, Michael tells Dennis they're going to hike up to the old mine.

Dennis grabs his sleeve and pulls him out on the front porch.

He says, "Is that lady high?"

"Yeah. Probably."

"That's so weird, man. What is she, like, sixty?"

"I guess. I didn't ask."

"Not to keep repeating myself or anything, but this is all very weird. But I guess you figure you know what you're doing."

Michael thinks a minute before answering.

"Well, no," he says. "Not really. But somebody does."

Dennis points a finger at Michael's chin. "Man, that's the first smart thing I ever heard you say."

· ★ ·

Michael shines a flashlight into the mine shaft cut into the steep side of the hill.

Mary Ann asks if the roof is strong.

"Oh, hell," he says, "this old mine's been here for sixty years. Maybe more. Been through earthquakes. Nothing's gonna bring it down."

"Are there bats in here?"

"Yeah, but they're sleeping. They're really harmless, you know."

She hooks her arm through his, and he's grateful for the feel of it against his side. They take one measured step after another. Into the damp darkness. That place he's never liked to go.

Michael says, "I know now why I brought you up here. I was always afraid of this place. I know why now. It was those caves."

"What caves?"

"You know. In the Pacific."

"Guadalcanal?"

"Right. *That* was the name of that place."

"Yes, but what's this about caves?"

The narrow shaft opens out into an irregularly shaped room. Michael shines his flashlight up to the ceiling. The bats are there, sleeping. They shift around as the light hits them.

"Don't wake them up, Michael."

He leans back against a wall, and she pushes close to his side. He breathes deeply, reminding himself he's not claustrophobic. That was Walter.

Mary Ann says, "Now tell me about those caves."

"Oh. Right. The caves. There was a mountain on that island, about six miles from the field. Whatever enemy was left when we got there holed up in caves. They were like arsenals. We had to blast out the entrances and rush them. They always knew we were coming. Their eyes were always better adjusted to the dark than ours."

"Oh, and you were so claustrophobic, too."

"Yeah, that too. Didn't anyone tell you any of this?"

"No, not a word. I just got small talk. 'The guys are great, the food stinks. The flies are driving us crazy.'" They both stare at the circle of light trained at their feet. "Michael? Was it very ugly the way he died?"

A pause before Michael answers.

"It's probably better I don't tell you. I don't think it's something you'd want to picture."

He hears the stress in her voice. Her volume comes up to match it. "I asked Andrew about that. He said no, it was just a little bullet hole in your forehead."

"Oh." He puts an arm around her shoulders. "He was probably just trying to help."

"I wish he wouldn't do that, though. I wish he'd give me credit for being able to handle things."

He pulls her close and kisses her forehead. "In his own misguided way he was trying to take care of you."

"I know."

He sinks down to the cool floor. Sits with his back up against the hard dirt wall. He sets the flashlight down so it shines across the cave. She sits close beside him.

She says, "Why did you come back? And why now, with so much time gone by?"

"Beats hell out of me."

They sit quietly for a time. Then he slips his hand around hers. It seems to break a tension between them. It seems to be what everything and everybody was waiting for. Even the bats sound calmer.

With the light aimed across the cave, the spot where they sit together is suitably dark. It's impossible to really see her. When he closes his eyes, he can see the way she looked in high school. At the train station, waving as he pulled away. He can see the face of Walter. He could even be wearing it, for all he knows. It could be his own face he sees so clearly in his head.

He says, "I never did do right by you."

"Don't ever say that."

"It's true, though. I didn't ever deserve you. I have so many regrets about that. I should have treated you better while I had the chance. You know what I regret the most? That night in my dad's car."

"You regret that?"

He hears cold fear in her voice. Fear he's said, or will say, something to revoke what little she has left, he assumes.

"Not that it happened. Just that it was so fast. And I was so bad."

"You were just nervous."

"Yeah. That's what I was about to say. But it was important to you. It was our only chance."

She reaches over him and turns off the flashlight. And he isn't surprised by that. He isn't surprised by anything that could happen now.

"So, make it up to me," she says.

· ★ ·

Michael wakes in the night and moves close to her. It's been so long since he's had a woman in his bed.

At first she feels strange against him. She feels old. Her skin seems to fit too loosely. Then he remembers who this is beside him, and the feeling evaporates. He allows himself to feel the warmth of another human being, of something that feels like caring.

She says, "I thought I'd had my last twenty-one-year-old man quite a few years ago." Her voice sounds young, familiar, and very much in place. It brings him home. Sets him back down in the earlier time.

He smiles at her, wonders if she can see his smile in the dark.

Then he falls asleep again.

· ★ ·

When he wakes, it's light.

He reaches for her, but she's gone.

On her side of the bed is a note.

Dear Michael,

I'm not a twenty-year-old girl anymore, as I'm sure you noticed. I'm almost three times your age. It was nice to ignore that reality for a couple of days, but we can't keep it away forever.

You asked me how I could go back to him, so I guess this is your answer. Without looking at your face on the way out the door.

I'm sorry about that part, but only that part.

Love,

Mary Ann.

For a few minutes he holds the note so tightly that it crumples in his hand.

He wonders when he last felt so bruising a sense of loss, and what he used to do to make it go away.

CHAPTER FIFTEEN

Andrew

He sits on the couch, his arms crossed, as he hears her car pull into the driveway.

He doesn't stand to meet her at the door. He always stands to meet her at the door. So that should serve as her first clue that something is amiss.

"Hello, dear," she says, and crosses the room to plant a kiss on his forehead. She does not betray whether or not she has picked up on the clue.

This irritates Andrew, makes him want to speed things up a bit, so he says, "How's Margaret?" He really cares nothing about Margaret, so that should be her second clue that he is wise to her.

"Fine, dear. Just fine. She sends her love."

She turns back to the desk and begins to sort through the week's mail.

"What day did you get in?"

She stops for a split second, glances over her shoulder, but not far enough to connect with his eyes. Did he give it away with his voice? Body language? Or is her own guilt enough, without his helping?

"I'm not sure I remember, dear."

"Well, how long was the drive? How many nights did you stop over?"

"Um. Let me see. It might have been two."

"So you didn't get in until Saturday."

"Saturday? Yes, I guess. That sounds right."

Emotionless, so far as he knows, he picks up her bag off the floor and begins to plow through it, tossing clothes onto the couch. He refuses to look at her face. He feels his anger harden and set, allowing him to be unreasonable without ever questioning himself.

He hears her say, "Andrew, what on earth are you doing?"

He most wants to find a slip of paper, an address, a map of a strange location. At this point almost anything would do. Almost anything left from the trip, even scribbled directions. He settles on her camera. That should get results.

He checks the counter to see three exposures left. He snaps three pictures of the carpet, then hears the whine of the motor as the film rewinds automatically.

He pops open the back and drops the roll into his palm.

She grabs for his hand, but he closes it into a tight fist around his prize. He knows he holds something of value now, because she doesn't want him to have it.

"Andrew, what on earth is wrong with you?"

"I called your sister's house Sunday morning. You weren't there yet."

Her eyes register a split second of alarm. Always watch the eyes. Something as true in love as in war.

"Okay, then I guess it was Sunday I got in."

"Four days to drive from Albuquerque to San Francisco?"

She takes a deep breath as if to steady herself, and that nicely unbalanced look in her eyes disappears. She pulls her shoulders up straight.

"Andrew, I insist you give me back my film."

"As soon as you tell me where you were."

He watches her count, sort, balance her options. She could trick or overpower him, but she won't. She respects his skills too much for that.

He supposes she could barter it off against the things he can't do for himself. He hasn't had a clean shirt or a decent meal for a week. But no, not immediate enough.

Come on, he thinks. Use your head. Take the short way home. Talk.

"I went to see Michael Steeb." Michael Steeb, Michael Steeb. Why does that name sound so familiar? "The young man who wanted to know about Walter."

"Oh, yes." He feels a turbulence build in his gut. He so wanted to remain unemotional. Now things are spinning out of control. "So, what does his point of interest turn out to be?"

"You wouldn't understand."

"In the two days or so that you were there, did he happen to mention why he came to the door and called you his girl?"

She holds out her hand, firm and unwavering. A deal's a deal, the gesture says. He drops the film into her palm. She turns away, walks into the bedroom, slams the door.

Every inch of his insides wants to go after her, pound on the door, break it down if she's locked it. He wants to scream, to release the tension from his gut, to feel clear again. To make her answer all his questions. Is this Steeb person crazy, or is he after something? Why in God's name would you trust him? Just how much of a betrayal is this? And if it isn't, why did it happen behind my back?

And why, would you please tell me, why aren't you talking to me?

Instead, he pours a glass of bourbon. Lights a cigarette.

He is not going to take it out on his wife.

He has never screamed at her, or broken her door down. Or questioned her loyalty. And he's not about to start now.

He rummages quietly in her open bag until he finds Michael Steeb's original letter, folds it once and puts it in his shirt pocket.

If he's going to ask questions, why not go straight to the man with the answers?

· ★ ·

Two and a half bourbons later, she emerges voluntarily.

"When he first came to our door," she says, "I'd never seen

him before. I didn't even know it was the man who had written. And he knew my name."

Andrew stares, curious as to the purpose of this seemingly pointless exercise. He notices something in her voice and manner that makes him want to handle her gently, like antique china.

"Well, honey, you wrote him a letter."

"I signed it Mrs. Andrew Whittaker."

"Well, even so. It's not too hard to find out my wife's name."

"Look, Andrew." She sits beside him on the couch. He watches her face, feels an unfamiliar sensation in his stomach, realizes he's frightened of what she's about to say. "I know this goes against everything you believe. But no matter what you call it, or how you try to explain it away, he remembers things that only Walter should remember. He told me about how you two used to borrow his dad's car and drive to Atlantic City. He told me about the caves on Guadalcanal, and the way you had to rush them. And you know what else? You lied to me. He said it wasn't just a bullet hole in his forehead. He says it's something I wouldn't have wanted to see."

Andrew averts his eyes, checks to see that his shoes are tied. He feels suddenly, uncomfortably, like a kid on his way to the principal's office. Because he has been caught in a lie, even if the sources of truth are highly suspect.

"Well now, I'm sure there's a good explanation, dear. I'm sure somebody we fought with fed him the information."

"But why? What would be the point?"

"I'm sure I don't know. But I'll bet you I can find out."

"No, Andrew. It's not a trick. I know this is very hard for you. But you have to trust me on this. You have to try. You know how you always tell me to look at the eyes?"

"Sometimes a con man can have very convincing eyes. Because they know that trick, too."

"No, Andrew. It's not just that his eyes are sincere. They're his."

"His?"

"Walter's. He has Walter's eyes."

Andrew feels a deep sorrow in his chest, like a balloon filling that will soon leave room for nothing else. He puts his arms around her and holds her close, presses his face against her soft cheek.

"I understand."

"You do?"

"Of course I understand. With all the grief you've been through, you're the perfect victim. I don't blame you. Not one bit. I blame him, all the way."

She pulls away, closes herself back into the bedroom. This time he hears the lock click into place.

CHAPTER SIXTEEN

Walter

Poor Andrew. He'd like you to think he has everything under control. He'd like everybody to think that.

If you ask him about his childhood, he'll say it was fine. It
was a disaster. I was there.

If you ask him about his dad, he'll say he respects his dad.
He'll neglect to mention that his dad would slap him halfway
across the room for anything that suggested even a whiff of
disrespect.

It's not even in what we say about ourselves, so much. It's
in what we leave out.

But I'm the one who doesn't buy any of these lines. Nobody can keep anything from me, because I was there. In fact, I'm there now.

I'm standing at Andrew's door. Knocking. Andrew's dad won't get a phone. He says he's not made of money. So when Andrew doesn't show up as planned, I have to walk over there and knock.

Andrew's dad comes to the door holding a beer. He's a strange-looking man. Whatever is not exactly handsome about Andrew, this is where it came from. He's a big man, if you consider height only. But he's skinny and really old. I think he was something like fifty when Andrew was born. Or something close to that, anyway. His chest is all sunken, and his hair is white and flies in a lot of directions at once.

I can't exactly read the look on his face, but he's not happy. Then again, when is he ever happy? He seems to be telling me something with that look, but it's not, "Please come in." It's not, "So happy you could join us."

He turns his back on me and walks away. Just walks away from the front door, leaving it standing wide open. Not a word has been spoken.

This is not normal. Even my house is normal compared to this.

I step inside and call Andrew's name.

He calls back from somewhere at the back of the house.

I find him in the kitchen with his mother.

"I can't leave now," he says, even though we had very specific plans for the day. "I have to stay and take care of my mom."

Andrew's mother is the shyest person on earth. It always

seems like it's going to kill her if she has to exchange one look or one word with anybody. Even her family. She looks like she's just going to roll right over and die.

She's at the kitchen table. Her hair is long and straight, starting to go gray, and it's all down in her face. Her head is down, so her hair is falling all across her eyes. I can't tell if there's something specifically wrong. I mean, something more than usual. When she glances up, her eyes look swollen, but maybe it's just from crying. I can't tell if she got hit.

Andrew pulls me aside. Pulls me to the far corner of the kitchen, off on the other side of the refrigerator.

"Can you wait here with my mom for a minute?" He's talking quietly, almost whispering. "I have to go to the store."

I can think of lots of things I'd rather do than sit alone in a room with Andrew's mother, including playing with rattlesnakes and dying.

"I'll go to the store," I say. "What do you need?"

"Aspirin for my mom, and something else, but you don't want to buy it, believe me. You'd be mortified. I don't even want to tell you."

Maybe I know what he means. I don't know for sure that I know, but I totally take him at his word on the mortification factor.

"Won't you be mortified?"

I look at his eyes and see that he is already. His eyes are begging me to stop witnessing all this. To give him back that dignity coat he puts on when he leaves the house. Stop seeing underneath it. No wonder he always comes to my house instead.

I say, "I'll wait here with your mom."

"Don't leave even for a second. Okay?"

"Okay."

I sit at the kitchen table with Mrs. Whittaker for five minutes or so. I'm looking at the big noisy kitchen clock, so I know it's only about five minutes. I would have thought it was more. She's careful not to look at me, and I'm extra careful not to look at her. The only words spoken so far have been between me and Andrew.

Then his dad comes in. Stops short and looks at me. Looks at his wife, who keeps her head down. Then back at me.

"You still here?" he says.

"Yes, sir."

"You can go now."

"No, sir, not really I can't. I promised Andrew I'd stay."

"Andrew's not even here."

"I know. He just ran to the store. I promised I'd wait."

"You can't wait on the porch?"

I notice that Mrs. Whittaker is looking at me from behind her hair. We catch each other's eyes for a split second. Then we look away as fast as we can.

"No, sir," I say. "I promised I'd wait right here."

He stands there a minute, chewing on his lip. I'm thinking probably I could take him. I'm thinking it might be about to come to that. I bet Andrew could take him. Thing is, I know that wasn't always true. That's the problem with parents like him. By the time you get big enough to take them, the damage is done.

He goes over to the refrigerator. Takes out a beer. Like that's all he really came for. Flips off the top. He's got a bottle opener mounted on the side of the fridge, with a waste can right underneath. He's got this down to a science.

Then he's gone.

Andrew gets back not five minutes later, all red and out of breath from running.

"I'll talk to you tomorrow," I say, and get out as fast as I can.

So far as I know, though, Andrew doesn't leave the house for three days.

Other times it's just the opposite. He gets stuck out of the house and won't go home. Won't or can't. What the difference is, I couldn't say. There are so many questions you just don't ask.

There's another time where he comes into my yard in the middle of the night and throws a basketball against the side of the house, right next to my bedroom window. As close as he can get to the window without breaking it. At first I just lie in bed and listen to it. Thump. Thump. Thump. I'm tired, so I'm pretending it has nothing to do with me.

After a while I put on my pants right over my pajama bottoms and go to the window. Sure enough, there's Andrew, waving to me.

I put on a sweater and go out to meet him.

"What the hell?" I say. "We got a track meet in the morning. What about sleep?"

"Walk with me," he says. "Let's go down to the beach."

It's hard to explain why I do. Something about the way he asked. Like I'm his last hope in the world for something. I don't know what. I don't want to know what.

We walk all the way down to the boardwalk. Sit on the

cold boards with our legs dangling over the edge. Leaning on the low rail. Not saying much. Just being out here with the night, hardly talking.

The sky is light with moon, and clouds are blowing around. Big dark clouds. They cover up the stars and then show them again. We can hear the rush of the ocean like something breathing in the dark.

Andrew says, "Let's stay and watch the sun come up."

"You're joking. We got a meet tomorrow. We have to sleep."

"Just do this one thing with me, okay? What's the worst that could happen?"

"I'll lose the hundred yard."

"For one time. Big deal. One time. Everybody loses once."

I really don't, though. I mean, not recently. Track is that one solid area of my life. That one thing I can really do. That place I don't lose.

But I sit there with him until that orange glow comes up on the horizon. The sun comes out of nowhere like it does every morning, only usually I'm too smart to be around to see it.

When we can see the whole round orange ball, I say, "That's it. We're going home."

"I can't," Andrew says. "I can't go home."

"Come to my house, then."

I slip him in the back door, and he lies down on the floor in my room. I sleep about an hour. I don't know if he sleeps or not.

Then my mom comes in to wake me up.

"Walter, get up, honey," she says, "you've got a meet to—" She sees Andrew and stops and just lets herself out again.

Andrew leaves through the back door.

My dad is waiting for me at the breakfast table.

"Did you go out last night?" he asks.

"Yes, sir."

My mom puts a stack of six pancakes on the table for me, with butter and syrup, and bacon on the side.

"In this house," he says, "we are not wild animals. We go out in the day and sleep at night."

"Yes, sir."

"I don't know or care how they do things at the Whittaker house, but at the Crowley home, we act like civilized human beings."

"Yes, sir."

"I trust nothing along these lines will happen again."

"No, sir."

But when Andrew needed me again, it would happen again. There comes an age when you answer a call that has nothing to do with the family that raised you. You grow up over their heads, beyond their reach. They'll hate you for it, but this is the natural order of things.

I'd reached that moment. Andrew and I both had.

We were just that close to grown.

I won the hundred yard all the same.

CHAPTER SEVENTEEN

Michael

Michael is awakened by a knock at his door. Dennis must be in town, or out in the fields, because nobody answers it.

He pulls on a pair of jeans and stumbles to the door. It's his mailman.

"Telegram."

"Thanks."

He closes the door and tears open the envelope. His hands shake. A telegram, he figures, is like a phone call at 3:00 A.M., if he had a phone. It smacks of bad news.

He reads it, can't decide if it's bad news or not.

EXPECT VISIT FROM ANDREW STOP HE LEFT WITH-
OUT SAYING WHY STOP HE TOOK YOUR LETTER STOP
THE CAR'S STILL HERE STOP HE MIGHT FLY STOP
MIGHT BE THERE SOON STOP WANTED YOU TO BE
PREPARED STOP LOVE MARY ANN.

He decides not to bother to try to sleep.

Instead, he drives into town, gets her number from long distance information, calls her from a pay phone on the corner. The town is waking up. Pickup trucks now and again cruise down Main Street, and each driver waves at Michael. And Michael, who would rather concentrate on what he's doing, must be a good neighbor and wave back.

Even though she said he's gone, Michael is still half prepared to hang up if Andrew answers the phone.

Mary Ann answers.

"Hey, it's me, Michael. I got your telegram."

"Oh, good. I was a little worried about you."

"Why, do you think he's, like, violent?"

"No, probably not. But he's not happy. He thinks it's a scam, and I'm your victim."

"Oh. Uh-oh. He always was very protective about things like that. Hey, Mary Ann . . ." He pauses, listens to her silence, wonders if she cares to interject. "I wanted to write, or call or something, but I was afraid it would just make a mess."

"I'm sorry I left without saying good-bye."

"I'm just sorry you left." Michael stares through the light traffic on Main Street, sees a man, a stranger, standing close to the booth, waiting to use the phone. He turns his face toward the back wall of the booth. "I mean, is that it? Now we just have to give each other up again?"

He taps his foot, waiting for her answer.

"I don't know, Michael. I think that's how it goes, yes. I mean, when you think about it—"

"Well, of course, if you think about it, but this doesn't have anything to do with thinking, right?" If we'd used our heads, he thinks, it never would have gone down that way. She doesn't answer. "So he just left in the night, or what?"

"Yes, he left a note saying he'll take care of it."

"Uh-oh. What did you tell him?"

"Not much. Just that you have Walter's memories. And his eyes. So. Um. Give me another call if you see him, okay?"

"Okay. Mary Ann? Before you hang up . . ."

"Yes?"

But he has no idea. He just doesn't want her to hang up. He just interjected that to postpone the process in which she rings off the line, leaving him back in his life alone and more than a little confused. As always, he has no real idea of what to say to her, yet he doesn't want her to go. And he doesn't exactly know why.

"Never mind. We'll talk some other time."

He hangs up the phone. Steps into the little corner market. Stands near the register, digging in his pockets for money. He only needs a loaf of bread. That's all he came in to buy. And he has two dollar bills and a handful of change, which should be enough.

But then his eyes light on the rack of cigarettes behind the counter. Lucky Strikes. He's never smoked cigarettes before to speak of. Oh, maybe a handful in high school, barely inhaled. But he feels he can taste that Lucky Strike smoke going down, and he can't live another day without it.

He doesn't have enough for cigarettes and bread, so he skips the bread.

He lights his first one out on the street. He's right. It tastes just the way he expected.

· ★ ·

Michael sits out on his upstairs balcony in the cool evening, feet dangling, shirt open, saxophone strap pressing his collarbone, almost as though he's trying to recreate that first night. But he knows this first night with Andrew will be different.

The music is a little off tonight, as if it's waiting, too.

Andrew shows up on foot. Michael sees him from quite a distance. Watches his progress in the heavy dusk. Notes how the walk is so familiar, even though the limp is not. Still, whether he'd known Andrew was coming or not, he'd have known him from a hundred paces off.

He must have flown, Michael figures from the timing. He must have walked nearly four miles from town. Maybe he thought there would be a bus. Maybe he didn't realize his destination was so far out in the sticks.

Andrew limps up to a spot in front of the house, as if to get a good view of Michael in the half darkness. Only then does Michael stop playing and let his sax rest against his chest.

"Andrew. I've been expecting you."

He looks down at his shape in the moonlight, feeling tall and strong because he's so far above him.

Earlier in the evening, he loaded Dennis's rifle, just in case. Then he decided he'd let Andrew kill him before it came to that. He probably couldn't shoot anybody, but he couldn't shoot Andrew even to save his own life.

Then, as an afterthought, he packed up all the contraband and handed it to Dennis with a request that Dennis spend the night elsewhere. When a man comes gunning for you, why supply the ammunition?

Andrew squints up at him, and Michael realizes Andrew's night vision is not good. He's not a kid anymore.

"I have a number of questions for you, Mr. Steeb." His voice sounds measured. He has obviously planned this moment carefully.

"Well, Andrew, I've got a bunch for you, too. And since this is my land, and you're technically trespassing, and I could ask you to leave at any time, let's do mine first."

"I don't promise to answer anything."

"I wouldn't say these are questions that need answers." He waits for an argument, but Andrew only stares. "Do you remember old Mrs. MacGurdy, from down the street? She was the one had that old cat. Angel, her name was."

He's rehearsed a few things, too.

"I remember Mrs. MacGurdy, but the cat's name was Henrietta."

"Henrietta? Andrew, where is your brain anymore? The cat's name was Angel. You remember, it was that real old cat, like twenty-one or twenty-two years old. She couldn't even climb steps. Mrs. MacGurdy had to carry her up and down the cellar stairs."

"I remember the cat. I remember she carried her up and

down the stairs. But I'm telling you the damn cat's name was Henrietta."

He feels tension, even anger, rise in Andrew's voice, and for a moment he almost rises to meet it. Then he steps outside the conflict, and it makes him laugh.

"Andrew, what the hell difference does it make what the cat's name was? This is not even about the cat. It's about the trick we played on Mrs. MacGurdy. We didn't tell anybody about that, remember?"

Does he catch a flicker of something in Andrew as that information settles in? It's hard to tell. It's always hard to tell with Andrew. He always keeps the most important things where you can't quite reach.

"Who's we, punk? You weren't even born. Your mother was barely born."

"You and Walter. Made a vow of secrecy, remember?"

For the first time since his arrival, Andrew looks down at the dirt.

Michael takes a deep breath, smells hay and fresh water, and decides that none of this must be taken too seriously. He has to step back and breathe. He has to let some parts of this be Walter's and not his.

"Well, you're good," Andrew says, his face coming up to watch again. "Whoever you're getting this stuff from, you really did your homework."

"Okay, here's another one. Remember this? We're sitting in a matinee, watching the cartoon. No one in the damn theater but you and me. And I turn to you and say, 'That's what I want to be.' And you say, 'What? A mouse?' And I say, 'No, not a mouse. An animator.' There was no one there to overhear, and I wouldn't have told that stuff to anybody but you."

"I really wish," Andrew says with mock politeness, "that you wouldn't talk about my friend Walter in the first person. You're not Walter, not by a long shot. And it disturbs me."

"Well, damn. I was just getting to like that." But he says it quietly and declines to repeat it. "Okay. Your friend Walter would not have told that stuff to anybody but you."

"That's what I would have thought. But I guess I didn't know him as well as I thought I did. I wish you'd come down from there. I'm getting a stiff neck."

"You're right, Andrew," he says as he sets the saxophone down on the wooden deck. "You didn't know him nearly as well as you thought you did."

He pushes off with his hands and jumps down from the balcony, landing with slightly bent knees on the dirt a few feet in front of his visitor.

Andrew jumps as if Michael had fired a shot.

"Well, you asked me to come down."

Michael walks up onto the downstairs porch and sits in an old rocking chair.

"Here's one more question, Andrew. Do you want to know why Walter hated that Purple Heart so much? Would you like to hear what really happened after the two of you got separated?"

"Not from you, I wouldn't."

Michael sighs and shakes his head.

"You, Andrew, are a stubborn, closed-minded old man. When I knew you, you were a stubborn, closed-minded young man."

"I don't have to stand here and be insulted."

"No, that's true, you don't. No one's holding a gun to your head." He realizes as he hears it that it's an expression he borrowed from Walter. He'd never said it until just now.

"Answer me one question, young man. Just one. If I am such a stubborn, rotten person, why did you go so far out of your way to find me?"

"Now that is a very good question, Andrew. I think it's because I love you in spite of yourself. And because we need each other. We're both stuck, and we need each other more than we know."

"You *are* crazy," Andrew says, and turns to walk away.

Michael closes his eyes, tries to picture Walter, tries to think how to find him on short notice.

Because he needs him now. Because they're on the brink of losing what they came so far, came through so much, to find.

Because Andrew is walking away.

"Excuse me," he says under his breath. "Walter? I'm dying down here. Are you going to help with this, or what?"

CHAPTER EIGHTEEN

Walter

For all the talk about Andrew's bravery and prowess, my own included, I was stronger than Andrew in a way that's subtle but important.

I will provide one open-and-shut example.

I'll tell you how I earned, or failed to earn, my infamous Purple Heart. I know I said I don't talk about that, but I changed my mind. I'm strong enough. Sometimes, I've decided, you just have to take your worst secret and put it on the table. Maybe it'll lose some of its power just sitting out there in the light.

Here goes.

Andrew and I belong to the army's 25th Infantry Division. What that means in layman's terms is that the real heroes, the 1st Marine Division, did the real work and got the real glory, whereas we come in like mop boys to clean up.

That's why Andrew calls this Anticlimax Island, in case you care.

It looks to be a cush assignment until we're told that a mere twenty thousand enemy troops are still hiding in or on the mountain. And Mt. Austen affords a view of Henderson Field, so you can imagine General Patch is anxious to get them boys out of there.

So they give us two days' training about fighting in caves, then send us packing. Six miles. We think, Not a bad hike. We will be proven wrong. But so far as we know now, this is not such a bad island.

All we've seen so far is Henderson Field, the beachhead, a little strip of the Lunga River. We see beautiful fields of tall grass, but we don't know it's kunai grass, which cuts like a saw-toothed blade when you try to push through it.

We don't know how it feels to wade chest-deep in ancient decay while mosquitoes eat us alive and a crocodile eats a buddy two steps ahead.

I myself have not guessed how a pair of legs can feel after slogging three miles of the distance in thigh-deep mud.

And then when we get where we're going, the flies want our K rations worse than we do. You have to flick them off each bite with your free hand, then get it to your mouth before they light again. You get the timing down after a while, but it's not easy, and if you miss a beat, it's not fun.

Then comes the part where Bobby gets killed and we camp the night, but I told you that already.

In the morning we draw straws to see which two lucky guys get to wait outside with the mortar. Hutch and Oscar get the prize. Now, this is quite a prize, because they get to stay out in the light, and if they see any enemy at all, it will be from a hundred feet away. In essence, they will be snipers. We get to be the sitting ducks. In the dark.

They get to aim a round at the cave entrance. This is step one. This is to open things up. Then all they have to do is pick up one end of the mortar each and run it a few paces down-hill. Then they guard the entrance, and if one of "them" comes out, they pick the guy off with their rifles. If one of "us" comes out, we're supposed to yell "Hutch!" real loud, so Hutch doesn't shoot us.

Now I ask you, is that so hard?

So we stand ready at the cave entrance, take off in threes. That way we're less likely to trip over each other in the dark.

Andrew and Jay stand to my left.

Our turn. We take off running.

Halfway in, something slams into me and knocks me off balance, like a body going the other way. It's pitch dark now, and I bump the sweaty wall, spin around. I don't know my directions anymore. For the first time since boot camp, Andrew and I are separated.

Maybe it's my claustrophobic imagination, but I think I can feel the coolness of the wall across from me, and the ceiling over my head, like it's all that close.

The panic rises up, and I feel like it'll choke me if I can't swallow it down again.

I hear sounds of struggle, voices, ours and theirs, but they seem to come from everywhere.

That's when I hear it. Jay's voice. I'd know it anywhere.

He shouts out a warning.

He yells, "Whit!" That's what they call Andrew. Whit.

And then the sound of a guy getting run through with a bayonet. Once you hear that sound, you'll never forget it. Trust me on that.

I think, That's it. Andrew. It's over.

Something in me breaks.

Maybe I should've prepared for this. I don't know. Some part of me must've known that Andrew could die at any time, and there'd still be a war to fight, and I'd be in it completely alone.

Maybe I should be prepared, but I'm not.

I run.

Don't ask me how I get back to the entrance, because I have no sense of my direction. I just follow two pairs of running footsteps and pray they know the way out better than I do.

And it works.

We come out into the light, and I see I'm running on the heels of two Japs. They don't seem to know I'm behind them. If they find out, I'm dead. All one has to do is turn around, and my life is over.

So I shoot them both. In the back.

And the minute I do, I hate myself for it.

Know why I do it, really? I mean, other than the obvious. I

could hang back in the cave in the dark to keep from being seen. But I shoot them. And I'll tell you a big part of why. Because I think if I don't, everyone will know. It's a case of skewed thinking, because there's nobody watching. Twenty feet farther down, Hutch and Oscar'll witness, but we're not twenty feet farther down. Everybody else is inside.

So it's not that I think anyone will see. It's that I think everyone will know. But it's too late now, anyway, because those Jap boys are dead and gone.

And I have to go back inside.

Okay, I panicked, I ran, but I'm out in the light and air now, and I know I have to go back.

Instead, I remember that Andrew's dead. Or so I believe. And then on top of that I pile two dead boys of my own creation.

So, what do I do?

I run like the devil's on my tail. Like I can actually run off that stinking island to someplace that isn't hell.

Only I make a big mistake. A huge mistake. I forget to yell "Hutch."

The bastard lobs a mortar round at me.

It's a hard thing to describe, getting hit by a mortar round. Or, more accurately, having one hit near the spot where you're standing. Or, as in my case, running like a cowardly fool.

It's a lot like flying, only more painful. I guess that's all I can say to explain. It just picks you up, and you ride along backwards on the cushion of air. Like a cross between flying and being hit by a truck. I don't recommend it. I landed a long way from where I was running, and that's all the memory I have for a good space of time.

There's quite a bit of speculation later as to why a mortar round. Why he didn't use the rifle as planned. Some say Hutch is just stupid, which God knows is true, and maybe at the last minute he forgot the difference between a rifle and a mortar.

I have to go with the ones who say he's plain mean. Kind of guy pulls wings off flies when he's a kid. Then he grows up and gets to shoot Japs, but he has more fun seeing if he can scatter them a little.

In a lot of ways, I hated him for it, but in one way, I was grateful. I take off like a coward in the line of duty, but nobody has to know. All they know is that I'm too stupid to yell "Hutch."

Yes, that is why "Walter hated that Purple Heart so much." Because, as Michael said, "I didn't earn it."

Doesn't sound like a story of strength yet, does it?

Maybe my idea of strength is different from yours, or anybody else's.

It's like this. I knew what I'd done, and I could accept it. It wasn't ideal, but it happened.

I could not have told Andrew. Because Andrew was not strong enough to take it. He couldn't have heard it. Or allowed it. He would have had to tell himself a story to keep it from being true, which is essentially what he did.

So, who's stronger, the man who looks truth in the eye, or the man who tells himself lies to make it go away?

He couldn't even face that my body was ruined. In fact, he

couldn't even let me face it. So I faced it while he was on duty, unable to hang around.

Andrew is not strong enough to face what he's about to find out. He'll have to grow into it while it's happening.

He'll want to look at Michael's eyes, because of what Mary Ann told him. As soon as he does, he'll know it's me. But he won't know he knows. Because he won't be strong enough yet.

When he knows he knows, then he can come home.

Then we'll all be free.

By the way, I'm not three days out of the hospital when I get my head blown off coming back from the mountain.

Makes me wish Hutch'd been a better shot. Save me a whole lot of trouble.

CHAPTER NINETEEN

Michael

Michael pushes up out of the rocking chair and calls Andrew's name. It seems far too easy, but it works.

Andrew stops, turns back.

Michael says, "That's it? You fly all the way from Albuquerque, get into town God knows how from the airport, walk all the way here—for what? Hear me out, call me crazy, leave? Not getting the most for your vacation dollars, buddy."

"I'm not your buddy. Crazy people are unpredictable. I don't like to be around them."

"No, me either. But, look, I'm pretty harmless, actually. I'm not going to hurt you."

"You hurt my wife."

"Really? How did I do that?"

"Got her believing you're Walter reincarnated, or his spirit popped into your body or something."

"Well, it's definitely one or the other. Walter says I'm Walter reincarnated and he should know. Why did you come here, Andrew?"

"To find out what your story is. What you're after. What kind of scam you got going."

"And have you done that to your satisfaction?"

"Not really, no."

"So . . . why are you leaving?"

· ★ ·

"Is this a house?" Andrew asks as he steps inside. "Is this on the way down or on the way up?"

"We're just building it, kind of a little at a time."

In the candle dimness, Andrew stoops to examine the dinosaur creature Dennis made out of mismatched fragments of driftwood. Michael can't tell if he thinks it's creative or insane.

Then Andrew sits on the mattress couch and looks around again.

"I guess it'll be a good house, when you're done. Kind of primitive now, though. Don't you even have light?"

"Not yet. That'll be a big expense. We're not electricians."

Andrew doesn't ask what comprises "we," as Michael expects him to. Michael is relieved. He's afraid if he mentions a nonpresent roommate, Andrew will think he's gay. That would only make things worse. Or would it? With Andrew's wife here behind his back, maybe it would help.

He says, "I'll light a lantern."

While he's working on that, Andrew says, "Do you at least have hot water?"

"Yeah, we have propane. We can shower. And cook. We're not wild animals, Andrew. We just can't afford an electrician for a little while."

When the lantern burns strongly, he sets it close to Andrew, to better see his face.

Andrew grasps it by the handle and sets it closer to Michael. He adjusts it slightly. It takes Michael a minute to realize what he's doing.

"You're trying to see my eyes, aren't you? To see if what Mary Ann told you is true?"

"How do you know what Mary Ann told me?"

Instead of answering, Michael holds the lantern up to his own face. Shines it on his own face so Andrew can see what he came here to see. Michael wants to see a reaction, but with the glare in his eyes, and Andrew's face in shadow, he's left to guess.

Andrew says nothing for an uncomfortable space of time. Then he says, "Oh, I get it. Walter went and had a kid we don't know about. That's why you've got those eyes. That's why you know so much."

"Andrew." He sets the lantern on the floor. "Wouldn't that make me about forty years old?"

Silence.

Then, "Oh, yeah. I'd know that, except I'm just so damned tired. I'm very tired. I'm going to go now."

"Why don't you sleep here?"

He lumbers to his feet. "No. No, I'm leaving."

"But you're tired. It's almost four miles back to town."

"I know how far it is as well as anybody. I just walked it."

Michael goes after him, catches him on the porch.

"There's a couple of motels in town. At least let me drive you in. You know, your leg."

Andrew pauses, looking purposefully the other way.

"Yeah, okay."

Michael lets him in on the driver's side of the van. The passenger door doesn't work right. He climbs in after him, hits the key, and the noisy engine coughs and runs.

"Don't you believe in mufflers?"

"Hey, quit chewing on me. I'm your ride."

"Yeah, all right."

They drive in silence for a mile or two.

Michael's trying to figure something about his invisible playmate, Walter. Like, where is he? Is he with him on this, or isn't he? Is he gone, or just so enmeshed with Michael's own insides that Michael can't feel him anymore?

"So, Andrew, maybe tomorrow morning I'll come by and take you to breakfast."

Andrew stares out the window, as though he can see something fascinating in all that blackness.

"Why would you do that?"

"Just so we can talk some more."

"I don't put much stock in talk."

"It can't hurt you, though. I mean, say I'm crazy, or just wrong. There's no danger in hearing me, and not believing a word I say."

"Okay, maybe. I'll call you."

"I doubt it. I don't have a phone. I'll just come by when I wake up."

He pulls into the parking lot of the Red Fox Motel. The sign says, VACANCY.

"So, first thing tomorrow, buddy."

"I'm not your buddy."

"Oh, yes, you are, Andrew. Fight it all you like, but you are my buddy."

"I'm just going to get some sleep," he says. "I'm very tired."

He tries to open the door, forgetting Michael has to let him out the driver's side.

Michael watches him limp into the lobby, thinking he looked and moved ten years younger on the path up to the house.

He thinks of finding a phone and calling Mary Ann, not so much because he said he'd check in, but because he needs to hear her voice.

But it's late, and he doesn't want to wake her.

He sits alone in the van, lights a Lucky, and blows smoke out the window in perfect rings, watching through the motel's front glass as Andrew registers.

He remembers the dreams that pushed him to find Andrew, the relentless nightmares that broke down his best resistance.

It hits him then that for Walter to help, Andrew will have to go to sleep.

Walter does his best work when you're asleep.

That fills him with a renewed sense of optimism. Maybe he really has done enough. Maybe Walter can be trusted to take it from here.

CHAPTER TWENTY

Andrew

Well into the night, Andrew hears the unmistakable sound of someone moving in his motel room.

Act like a soldier, he thinks.

Once he would have handled this. He would have startled awake with his brain sharp, ready to stay alive. Sprung into action. Jumped from zero to a hundred percent response in under a second.

Is he too old, or just too sleepy? His brain is filled with cobwebs and mush, his limbs with concrete.

He's going to die here, in this strange place. Why did he even come?

He sits up and turns on the light. The last thing a decent soldier would ever do.

In the chair beside the bed is Walter. Walter sets his elbows on his knees, leans in close.

A few strands of hair fall onto his forehead, and he brushes them back again, combing them into the bulk of his tousled hair with his fingers.

He's about twenty-one years old. He looks just as he did when Andrew last saw him alive.

His beard is grown out into stubble, his uniform is caked with mud, ripped in all the right places. Shoulder, pocket, lapel. His smile is familiar.

He says, "Hello again, buddy."

"Are you going to hurt me?"

Walter flops back in his chair and shakes his head mournfully. His eyes roll up to the ceiling.

"Cripes, Andrew, that's exactly what you said last time. Can't you learn some new lines?"

"What do you want? Why are you here?"

"Some greeting, buddy. I came to give you some information. See how much you appreciate it. Remember when I told you to check Mary Ann's whereabouts? You still haven't thanked me for that."

"Might have been better if I hadn't known."

"Andrew, Andrew, Andrew. You are such a disagreeable old man. You make it so hard to help you. Stubborn. Closed-minded."

"So I've been told. So why even try?"

"That, Andrew," he says, "is a very good question. I think

it's because I love you in spite of yourself. And because we need each other. More than you know, buddy. Anyway, here's what I came to tell you: It's all true."

"All what?"

"You know. What Mary Ann's been trying to tell you about Michael Steeb."

"She's a very emotional woman."

"You don't say that like it's a good thing."

"Me, I don't sell quite so easy."

Walter nods thoughtfully, a faraway look in his eyes.

"Okay, fine, buddy. Then we do it the hard way. I was just trying to save you the trouble."

Now the chair is empty, the room quiet.

· ★ ·

Andrew opens his eyes. He's not sitting up like he thought he was. The light is not on.

"Just a dream," he says out loud, as though someone besides him needs to hear it and believe it.

He rolls over, turns on the light, looks carefully around the room.

Satisfied, he turns off the light and falls back into sleep.

· ★ ·

In his new dream, he knows it's a dream, even as it happens, and that comforts him.

He sits on the end of the pier, feet dangling.

Walter sits beside him, in those white ducks he always wore, and a white short-sleeved shirt, with a pack of Luckies rolled into the sleeve.

It's spring, barely warm, with a good crisp wind up, and it catches in his shirt like a balloon, flapping and billowing.

The seagulls circle over their heads, and Walter throws them bits of stale bread from a brown paper bag.

"Hey, look at that," Andrew says, and points to a new car parked on the boardwalk. It's one of those jobbers with a split rear window, the first they've seen. It's too far away to read the make.

"Dodge," Andrew says.

Walter laughs at him, spitting the sound out between his lips like a Bronx cheer. "Plymouth. Betcha."

"Care enough to go look?"

"Hell, no." He tosses another scrap of bread, and the gulls scream as they dive for it. "Hear that?"

"What?"

"Hear what they said?"

"Yeah. They said, 'Squawk.'"

Walter shakes his head in disgust. "You don't listen right. Hey, Andrew, do you believe in reincarnation?"

"No, of course not."

Walter smiles broadly, slaps Andrew on the back.

"You will."

The slap brings him fully awake, the words ring in his ears as his eyes pop open.

· ★ ·

Andrew wakes, checks his watch. Five-thirty.

At six he calls the local bus company to find out when the first bus leaves for the airport.

At 7:15 he's on it, headed for home.

CHAPTER TWENTY-ONE

Walter

My mom's name is Millie, and I'm her favorite. And every-body knows it. My dad, Robbie, Katie. People we barely know. She really doesn't make much of a secret of it.

There's a special kind of guilt that goes along with that. You find yourself gearing your whole life to how you can make it up to somebody. I'll give you an example of what I mean.

Here's where I am.

I'm walking home from downtown with Andrew. I'm about sixteen. A sophomore. It's winter, and we just had a good, deep snow. It's still white and beautiful. It doesn't make a sound when you step into it. Not even a whisper. It's very fine and dry.

We're talking about sports, football to be exact, rubbing our hands together and watching our breath come out in frozen clouds.

Then we see some little kid getting picked on by two bigger kids. They're on the elementary school lawn, or what would be the lawn if it were summer. Then we see that the little one is a girl. Then we see it's my sister, Katie. She's got two boys ganging up on her, and one of them just hit her so hard in the back with a snowball that she fell into the snow on her face. Or maybe she tripped trying to run away. It's hard to tell at a distance. I guess this kind of snow doesn't make snowballs that knock you down. Anyway, she's down. Now one of the boys is holding her down and the other is rubbing snow in her face, pushing it down the collar of her coat.

It burns me. You know?

So I go off after them. One of the boys sees me coming. One I get to take by surprise. The first kid heads out entirely, gets a good running start. The other squirts out from under my hands and tries to run, but he trips and falls flat on his face. Now that's justice. I pick him up by one foot.

Maybe I haven't mentioned it yet, but my brother, Robbie, and my sister, Katie, are a lot younger than I am. Six and eight years. It's like my mother was satisfied to just have me. Then, I don't know. My dad wanted a bigger family, or they could have been accidents. You don't really ask a thing like that.

Anyway, Katie's the baby, and this boy who's picking on her is her age, and about half my size. So I grab him by the ankle and pick him up upside down.

His boot slips right off, and he starts to fall back onto the ground on his head, but I catch him again. Good save, right? So I'm holding him upside down by one skinny ankle with just a thin white sock on it.

I dip his head down into the snow. He tries to pull up, get his head out, and he blows the powdery stuff out of his nose and mouth.

"Pick on somebody your own size," I say.

"Yeah, same to you," he yells.

Sorry to say, he's got a point there.

I lay him down in the snow on his back and let go.

"Pick on anybody you want," I say. "So long as it's not my sister."

He gets up and runs away with this funny gait, this sort of peg-leg limp, leaving two distinct kinds of footprints in the snow.

I'm still holding his boot in one hand, this red snow boot with a fuzzy lining. I wedge it into the low crook of a tree so he'll see it when he comes back.

Then I go to help Katie up, but she's on her feet already, shaking the snow out of her coat. If looks could kill.

"You okay, Katie?"

"I can take care of myself, moron."

"Yeah, you were doing real well, there. I noticed."

"I hate you," she says, and stomps away.

I turn around, and Andrew is standing behind me.

"I'm so glad I'm an only child," he says. "Why do you even try with her?"

"Because she's my sister."

"She hates you."

"She doesn't hate me."

"She just said she hates you."

"She doesn't hate me. She hates everybody."

"You're part of everybody."

"She hates me less than most people."

"That's very touching," Andrew says. "Can we go home now? I'm freezing."

Okay, now back to what I was saying about my mom.

I get home, and she's made lemon pie for me. I can smell it. And I don't even know what the occasion is. Maybe there is none. Seems like the older I get, the closer I get to being a man, the more any old occasion will do. Like she needs to keep doing more and more just to break even.

Robbie and Katie hate lemon pie. They like apple, cherry, just about every pie ever made, but not lemon. They wrinkle up their noses when they smell it, and my mom says, "It's for Walter." Like they didn't know.

Now do you see why I owe them so big?

"Sit down," she says. "Take your boots off. It's just cool enough to cut."

There's some kind of look on her face that's vaguely troubling. Like a cloud just behind her eyes.

My mother is a beautiful woman. Not beautiful like the girls in Hollywood, but beautiful in a way that affects just about everybody who sees her. People stare, and it makes her uncomfortable. She has a way of turning her face down and away when people stare. She has a long, perfectly chiseled chin, and big dark eyes, and wavy hair that she sweeps back into a bun over the nape of her neck. But I think it's the smile more than anything else. The smile gets people. She doles it out very seldom, though. It's a small blessing that you have to enjoy while you can.

No smile today.

"What's wrong, Mom?" I ask, and I sit down at the table.

"Bud Gunderson called and said you roughed up his little boy. I told him I couldn't imagine you'd do such a thing."

"He was picking on Katie. I didn't rough him up. I just dipped him in the snow. He was picking on Katie. I was just teaching him a lesson."

She nods, kind of gravely. Now she has the cloud of Katie behind her eyes, too. She sets a piece of pie onto a plate for me. It's about a fifth of the pie. Probably weighs a pound.

"He says you took one of his galoshes."

"It came off. I left it where he could find it again."

She hands me a fork, silent. There's always something important in her silence, and she's silent most of the time. You find yourself listening hard to that silence. I wonder if she's ever really happy. She acts as if the only thing that makes her happy is me.

I say, "If you want, I'll go get the boot and take it over to his house."

She sits at the table with me. Shoulders rounded forward. Shakes her head. "No, if he was picking on Katie he can go back and get it himself. I just worry about what your father will think of all this. You know how he is."

I nod that I do, yes. I know how he is.

She says, "Maybe it would be better if we just didn't tell him about this. I'm thinking we just won't. It just never happened as far as I'm concerned."

I eat one bite of pie. It's the best thing in the world. It always tastes just the way I thought it would.

I ask her if she thinks Katie is okay.

Right away I can see I've made a mistake.

"Of course," she says. "She has a nice house, a family who loves her. Why wouldn't she be okay?"

In her eyes, I see I've really threatened her, challenged her, by raising the bar on okay. Here mothers are losing children every day, to accidents or illness. Watching them turn into juvenile delinquents. Mothers in Europe are losing their sons in the war. And my mother's children are home, in a warm house, fed, accounted for. And I have to go and suggest that there's more to being okay than that.

"I just worry about her sometimes," I say.

I worry about Robbie, too, but less. Because Robbie isn't afraid to ask for what he needs.

"Eat your pie, Walter," she tells me.

I do as I've been told.

That's the last time I try to rescue Katie. Probably I should have done more.

CHAPTER TWENTY-TWO

Mary Ann

About four hours after Andrew has come home and then gone again, her phone rings.

It's Michael.

He says, "Is Andrew home yet? Can I talk to him?"

"No, he's gone. I mean, he *was* home. For a minute. But now he's gone again. He said he needed a vacation. Needed to get away. Alone. It's not at all like him. He was shaken up. What happened, Michael?"

"Well, not much that I could see. I told him some things I remember, and he said I was a good con man. Then he looked in my eyes and started saying he was tired. We were supposed to have breakfast, but he took off. Did he say anything to you?"

"Just one thing. He said it's not a scam. He says you really believe it."

"But not that he does?"

"No, of course not."

A silence falls that feels oddly personal, considering no personal words have been exchanged.

She stares at the photo on the table, two crazy people on a rough, unpainted porch, their clothes covered with dirt and grease. Crazy lady who doesn't seem to know she's over sixty, her hair all slicked back, smiling like a kid. A stoned kid.

He breaks the silence. He says, "Can I see you? I really need to see you."

This ties in with something she had intended to say. Something she would have called to say, if he hadn't called her first.

She says, "I'm going to send you a plane ticket."

"No, save your money; let me drive."

"I'm going to send you a plane ticket to New Jersey. I'll try to get a flight close to the same time. I'll meet you at the airport. I'll send the ticket overnight mail."

"Why, what's in New Jersey?"

"Someone I want you to meet."

"Okay, fine. I'll go anywhere. I just want to see you."

· ★ ·

When she steps off the plane at the airport and walks to the gate, he's waiting for her, blended into the crowd as though this is home, and he's been waiting for her to come home again.

He hands her a bouquet of flowers. She doesn't know if he brought them from California or bought them at the airport gift shop. She feels shy and embarrassed over the gesture, but somehow pleased at the same time. She wishes he hadn't done it, but she's glad he did.

He throws his arms around her and doesn't let go. She feels the real sensation of his need, as though he's holding a life support. It's the way she used to feel about Walter. It's the way she used to wish Walter would feel about her.

He tries to kiss her on the lips, but she turns her face and presents her cheek. She motions to the crowd of people milling by, and he looks surprised to see them.

"Okay, right," he says.

But he seems disappointed.

She gives him a quick hug and then breaks away. She recognizes that familiar lump in his shirt pocket. It's a pack of cigarettes. She pulls it out to look.

Lucky Strike.

"Since when?" she asks.

"Not exactly sure," he says. "It snuck up on me."

· ★ ·

In the cab, Michael says, "I'm worried about him."

"Which him?"

"Andrew."

"Me too. But there's nothing we can do. Just let him work it out on his own."

"Who are we going to see?"

"Millie Crowley. Do you know who she is?"

He nods numbly. She can see that he knows.

"I thought it might be your last chance, so I'm rushing this a little. I want to warn you about a couple of things. She's almost completely blind. And she's not coherent most of the time. Sometimes she'll know who I am, sometimes she won't. She doesn't look good. I just want to prepare you."

Michael says nothing. Just nods, stares out the window until the nursing home comes into view.

Then he says, "That's the place, isn't it?"

She isn't sure why he says that, or how he knows.

· ★ ·

She straightens his collar just outside the room, then wonders why she did. Not for Millie, certainly. Just as a way of shoring him up, somehow.

He takes her hand on the way in the door.

Millie lies in bed, plastic tubes hooked into her nostrils. Her hands rest limply on the thin blanket. Mary Ann is prepared for this. She hopes Michael is, too.

Millie's weight is down again. Now she weighs maybe ninety pounds or less. Her skin is parchment, almost translucent, her arms just bone width, her hands bent with arthritis.

She looks to the door as if she will see.

"Hello, Millie," Mary Ann says. "I brought you a visitor."

"Who've you got there?"

Mary Ann elbows Michael gently in the ribs, prodding him

to speak. He doesn't seem to want to speak up. She thinks maybe he doesn't know what to call her.

"Hello, Millie," he says.

"Is that Walter? Is that my boy? Since when do you call me Millie? Come over here and sit down, son."

He lets go of Mary Ann's hand and walks to Millie's bedside, sits on a plastic chair.

"Hi, Mom. I wasn't sure if you'd remember me."

"How can you say that?" Her eyes stare right through him. "Why would you even say such a thing? A mother doesn't forget her own son. Who's that with you, dear?"

"It's Mary Ann, Mom. Don't you remember? My girlfriend."

"Oh, yes. Mary Ann." She fumbles for some grasp on him, finds his arm, pulls him close and whispers in his ear. But it's a loud stage whisper, and Mary Ann hears perfectly. "I don't know what you're waiting for, but hurry up and pop the question. While she'll still have you. You can't expect a girl to wait forever."

"I did, Mom. I gave her a ring and everything."

Mary Ann feels a tightness in her chest.

Millie's face lights up in a smile. That smile. It really hasn't changed all that much.

"Well, then this is a cause for celebration. I want grandchildren, right away. Three or four. Where are you?" She reaches out one skeletal hand to touch his face, running it over the top of his head, across his cheek, over his jaw. "Don't cry, son. Don't cry, Walter."

He does have a long trail of tears on each cheek, but he brushes them away again, as if they were a secret she was never meant to know. He takes hold of her hand in both of his.

Her other hand continues to explore his head. "You need a haircut, Walter."

"I know, Mom. You're right. I'll get one as soon as I get home."

He leans his upper body across her bed in a sort of loose horizontal hug, and she throws her bony arms around his back.

"Are you eating right? You're so skinny. That new wife of yours will have to put some meat on your bones. I'll have to teach her to cook. She'll have to take some of my recipes. You're used to eating right. She'll have to learn."

Mary Ann wants to close her eyes and try to see the world as Millie sees it. She wants to watch them all day. But she also feels that they deserve to be alone together in this moment.

She slips out of the room.

In the hall, she sees a familiar nurse, who hands her a Kleenex.

"What's the matter, Mrs. Whittaker, is she having a bad day?"

"No, no," she says, blowing her nose. "I think she's having a good day."

CHAPTER TWENTY-THREE

Michael

Michael looks up to see that Mary Ann has left the room.

He looks down at Millie again. Her smile has faded now, and another old familiar look has clouded her face. She's slipped back into that quiet seriousness that he remembers so well.

"Walter," she says. "They told me you were killed in the war."

"I was, Mom."

"Oh. That's right. I'm glad you're here, though."

"Me too."

"I'm going to die soon, too, you know." She says it almost proudly. "Did you know that?"

"Yeah, Mom. I know that."

The door opens, and a nurse comes into the room. A heavy, fiftyish woman with a seasoned face.

"Time for your sponge bath, Mrs. Crowley."

She says it with a mock cheeriness, a tone that doesn't sound genuinely happy. Or for that matter, genuinely anything. It's a tone one would use speaking to a child, and it makes Michael angry to hear someone talk to his mother that way.

"Not now," Millie says. "Can't you see Walter is here?"

"Walter?" The nurse looks Michael up and down. "I guess she thinks you're her son."

Now Michael feels the resentment build, because this stupid, thoughtless woman is talking right in front of Millie, as if Millie can't hear or understand. Nobody treats his mom like that.

"He *is* my son," Millie says.

"Yes, dear, of course."

"I *am* her son," Michael says. "The bath can wait. We're having a visit here." It feels like a remarkable accomplishment, to speak so calmly.

She eyes him a moment, as if deciding whether to rise to his tone. Then she says, "You got an hour. Then visiting hours are over."

Actually, he sees by the clock he has an hour and ten minutes, but he doesn't argue. He just lets her leave.

As soon as she's gone, he sits on the edge of Millie's bed. It's not a big bed, but she's so tiny and thin, she doesn't take up much of it. He slips off his tennis shoes, then stretches out by her side, easing her head onto his shoulder.

"Are you afraid?" he asks.

"Maybe a little. Should I be?"

"No."

"Will you tell me about it?"

"Sure. I'll try."

He's not really sure what to tell her, so he tries to fall back on Walter. Tries to let Walter be the one to speak. For the moment, that's who he'll need to be. Not some strange combination of both of them. Just Walter.

"It's a lot like what you've been doing already," he says, "except nothing hurts. And you can see a lot more. You can see everything that's happened or will happen, no matter where it is in time, and it all fits together. There's not one thing in the world that doesn't make sense. And all the things you thought were so important, they're just not a big deal anymore. It's like everything is important and nothing is important, but the things you always thought were important, well, they're just gone. I mean, they're there, but they don't mean a thing."

"That sounds nice."

"There's something to be said for it."

"What else?"

"Well, let's see. You're still you, but not the same you as before. A bigger you. And even though you didn't know that person, that bigger you, before, it definitely feels like you."

"And *you're* there, Walter?"

"I'm anywhere you want me to be, Mom. I mean, I'm here, aren't I?"

"Will you stay until I go to sleep?"

"Sure, Mom. I'm right here."

Michael closes his eyes, then opens them and looks at the clock again. They have more than an hour of visiting time left. And if she doesn't fall asleep within that hour, he'll keep his promise to her all the same. They're not getting him out of here until she's sleeping. Just let them try.

He tries to breathe around the lump in his throat, the anvil in his chest.

Her head feels light on his shoulder. She seems to weigh less than a whole person somehow. It makes him want to cover her like a shield. He listens to her breathing.

He thinks about a time when Walter was small. It's a time he's never thought about before. Until he was three or four, Walter was terribly shy. When someone came to the door, he would hide.

And this was a time when a lot of people came to the door. The milkman. The iceman. The Fuller brush man. Encyclopedia salesmen. There was a sense of interaction with the world that started right at your own front doorstep.

But that's a lot for a three-year-old boy. Sometimes he'd hide under the table, sometimes in the closet. When the knock came at the door, Millie would turn to him, her face all lit up and happy, helping him out by making it a game.

"Where should we hide this time?" she would ask.

Sometimes he would point to a place. Behind the couch, maybe. Other times he would wait for her suggestions.

Then, when the visitor had gone again, she would come find him.

"All gone," she'd say. "Come out, come out, wherever you are."

Once the iceman came to the back door and caught them by surprise, so she wrapped Walter up in her big skirt.

"Where's Walter?" he heard the iceman say, as if he really had disappeared.

Millie protected him from the world. Covered him like a blanket to make him feel safe. She knew he was safe, but he didn't. So she shielded him from his fears. Maybe every child starts out that way, he thinks. And then, unless that child dies young, he will live to return the favor. Then again, Walter died young. Maybe even that doesn't spare you from the moment when the roles shift on their wobbly axis.

He hears Millie's breathing broaden and deepen. It crosses his mind that she might be doing more than just falling asleep. But in just a few moments she begins snoring lightly.

He stays with her anyway.

He stays until Mary Ann slips back into the room. She stands at the door and watches. He almost thinks she'll disappear again. She seems uncomfortable, as if she's witnessing something she has no right to see.

Michael smiles to put her at ease, and they hold each other's eyes for a long time. Longer than they have since Michael arrived today. Maybe longer than they have since 1942. Maybe longer than they ever did.

Millie's snoring has calmed now, but Michael can still feel her breath against his neck.

Mary Ann says, "Is she . . ."

Michael puts a finger to his lips. "Sleeping," he whispers.

He gently slides his shoulder out from underneath her. Sits up on the edge of the bed and puts his shoes back on. Then he kisses Millie lightly on the forehead.

"We can go now," he says quietly to Mary Ann. "I think we're done here."

He looks back over his shoulder once. One long last look.

He hadn't been there when his own mother died, his this-life mother. He had been so young, and it hadn't seemed real. And it had made him feel restless to sit by her bed, so he'd stepped out of the room.

He keeps his head down on the way out, so all these strangers won't see he's been crying.

CHAPTER TWENTY-FOUR

Walter

Here's where I am. It's 1942. I'm in the kitchen with my mother. Only she doesn't see me. And she doesn't hear me. But she knows I'm here. She doesn't completely know that she knows I'm here. Part of her does. That part of her is enjoying my company, all the while stubbornly refusing to ask questions.

Then the knock comes at the front door.

She closes the swinging kitchen door and sits down at the table. Closes herself into the kitchen alone. Unless you count me, that is. She swings the door closed fast, and jumps back from it. Like it's going to bite her, what's on the other side of that door.

She's right. It is.

She lets my father be the one to get the door. Gather the news. Because, you see, that same part of her that knows I'm here also knows about that knock at the door. Because I can only be here if the news at the door is very bad. The worst news there is.

Another good example of a person seeing a great big chunk of forest. It happens.

She sits straight and tall, waiting. Her face is tight. I think she's looking for some power in herself she never knew she had. Looking for some way to make this not be true.

After a couple of minutes of this, my dad comes in. It's all right there on his face. So she doesn't look at his face. He walks over to her. Tries to touch her shoulder. She won't let him. She shoots out from under his hand. Paces back and forth a few laps on that tired but clean linoleum.

My dad does not know I'm here. My dad is not capable of knowing I'm here. It's just not who he is.

"Millie," he says. I wonder if he wonders over the fact that she seems to already know. "Millie," he says again.

She shakes her head.

No.

"Millie, it's about Walter."

She crumples, like she's about to faint.

Know what I do? I try to catch her.

I still haven't adjusted yet. It's not an easy adjustment to make. You think you have a body. You had a body for twenty-one years. It got to seem natural. Now you're back in the kitchen, trying to do a simple thing like break your mother's fall. Good luck, son. You're dead. Get used to it.

My dad catches her and helps her sit down at the table again.

"Millie," he says.

This time she says it out loud. "No."

"I have to tell you this."

"No."

My dad is crying. I never saw my dad cry. I never thought I would. It wasn't even on my list of possible things.

"Millie," he says, "it's—"

"No!" She screams it this time. Screams it so loud that he jumps away. She puts her hands over her ears now, so she can't hear any more.

My father gives up and leaves her alone.

Her head drops down onto the table.

I cover her with myself.

See, if I have no body, I can be any shape I want. I can take up any amount of space I choose. I can be a blanket. Drape myself over her like a down comforter. I can pour myself over her head like water. I can shine on her like light, bathe her with myself until she feels something resembling warmth again.

Don't believe it entirely, Mom, I say. I am not dead and gone. It's only half true.

I cover her for a long time. Days. I cover her until I know she'll survive.

Now the scene changes. I'm still in the kitchen with my mom, but it's different. We're both sitting up, at opposite ends of the table, looking at each other. The mood feels silky and calm.

The room is the same and yet not the same. We're not really here. That's the thing about this other side we're on. There is no landscape. If you want to see things in any kind of context, you have to pick a context. You have to take one from home. In this one, Millie is about forty. There are an infinite number of windows into this scene. I guess this is the one we've chosen.

She's not eighty. She's doesn't have to be eighty forever. She doesn't have to be anything forever. Nobody does.

The kitchen is washed with a kind of whiteness. It's bright, but the light is easy on the eyes. Of course, these are not really our eyes.

It's a good handful of days after Michael went to see her at the nursing home.

She says, "Walter. They told me you were killed in the war."

I say, "I was."

"Oh. That's right."

Then we just sit still together, letting the whiteness of things pour through us. A few minutes, a few years. It's hard to tell. It's hard to care. A while.

"It doesn't seem as important now," I say, "does it?"

Every line has left her face. Her eyes have no clouds. The clouds have parted. Not even a shadow to suggest they were once there.

"It seems important," she says. "It just doesn't seem wrong."

"See, I tried to explain it to you. But it's hard."

"You did fine," she says. "I understood everything you said. You were right. Everything you said about dying was true."

"Years of experience," I say.

This is one of the advantages of dying young. Everybody you left behind will need your help someday. You learn all these useful skills that everybody will need. Sooner or later.

CHAPTER TWENTY-FIVE

Michael

He stares out the cab window, watching an unfamiliar city flash by.

"Is this where we lived all those years? I don't recognize it."

"Everything's changed," she says. "A lot changes in forty years. Tomorrow I'll take you down to the boardwalk. That might help."

"Mary Ann? Does my voice sound like his?"

"No," she says. "No, it's not that. You have a way of talking like he did, but his voice was lower. I don't think it was any mistake on her part, if that's what you're getting at. It's not just that she can't see. I think she knew you."

He breathes deeply, smells ocean, lets out the air in a sigh.

"Let's hear it for people out of touch with reality. What would we do without them?" He combs his hair with his fingers, thinking maybe he really will get a haircut. "That's Andrew's problem. He puts too much stock in reality."

But there's more to what just happened than Millie's being out of touch with reality, and he knows it. She was also close to the other side. Maybe even close enough to see things most people can't. Plus all the barriers that might have kept her from believing such a thing were gone: her sound mind, even her own eyes.

They pull into a motel parking lot, and Mary Ann pays and tips the driver. Michael wishes he'd brought money, but what money would that be?

"Just so you know," she says on their way into the lobby. "I'm getting two rooms. That's *my* concession to reality."

He tries to argue, but it's too late. The manager greets them.

"Two rooms, please."

"Oh, no," Michael says, very sincere, "save your money. I don't mind being crowded."

She turns and shoots him a burning glance, hands her credit card across the counter. "The *reality* is," she says, "we can afford two rooms."

Michael shakes his head in defeat.

· ★ ·

He walks her to her door, gets his shoulders in before she can close it behind her.

He says, "Why are you doing this? Why can't I be with you?"

"I told you."

"Can't I even come in and talk?"

Her face softens. "Yes, of course."

He steps in after her, takes her in his arms.

"Don't, Michael," she says, and tries to pull away.

"I just want to hold you."

She relaxes gradually in his arms. He breathes against her ear, feels her chest rise and fall against his. He's only holding her, not attempting to transgress. But in one sudden movement, she slips away again.

"No, this won't work," she says. "We won't be satisfied to leave it at that."

"Then let's not leave it at that."

"I can't do this, Michael."

He sees the pain in her eyes, and he wants to make this easy for her, but his own pain rises up to overpower him.

"Why?"

"You know why."

"No. Tell me."

"Because I'm married to him."

He grabs her right hand, holds it up in front of her face, so the ring is right under her nose. Walter's ring.

"I asked you first," he says.

And he's angry about that. Genuinely angry. And he realizes that he has been for forty years. He just didn't know it until now.

He sees tears form in her eyes, but they don't make it as far as her cheeks. He waits for them to spill over, but they don't.

"I know," she says. "I know that, darling. But sometime in the last forty years you lost your place in line. I know it's not fair."

He tries to pull a chair away from the little table, but it doesn't go smoothly enough, so he ends up throwing it over onto the rug, half on purpose.

"You're worried about betraying him. But you don't think it's a betrayal when you leave me to go back to him. You don't see how that makes me feel."

"I do see. And I know how it makes *me* feel. I just don't know what I'm supposed to do about it. If I had known I'd ever have another chance with you, I could have made plans. Gotten a divorce."

"It's not too late."

"Oh, Michael, listen to yourself. Look at us."

She motions toward the mirror over the dresser. And their image in that mirror. And the reality it mirrors back to them. All the fight goes out of Michael. He can feel it pouring out, as if the plug had been pulled. He can no longer hold water.

She steps close to hold him again, but now he stands rigid in her arms, angry and unsettled.

"You're not using your head, dear," she says.

"No, of course I'm not," he says. "I'm using my heart."

But he carefully avoids the image in the mirror.

He kisses her briefly on the lips, then goes on to his own room.

· ★ ·

They stand at the railing of the boardwalk, looking out to sea. Michael feels that sense of familiarity he'd been missing. Something about the temperature and quality of the air. The saltiness of it. The way the wind flaps in his shirt. The line of ocean where it meets the horizon. Forty years can't change that. Maybe a thousand years couldn't change it. He's beginning to appreciate things that don't change.

"This is where you stood when he proposed to you, isn't it?"

"No, that was at the train station."

"I'm talking about Andrew."

She turns her face to him, and he watches her hair part and blow across her face the way it always did.

He pulls a Lucky out of his pocket and lights it, cupping his hands to shield the flame against the wind. The hot smoke satisfies him in a deep and ancient way as he pulls it in.

"How do you know where Andrew proposed to me?"

"I was there."

She stares out across the waves in silence.

Then she says, "I knew that. I felt it. Until after we got married. Then I couldn't feel you there anymore."

"I stayed until my kid brother joined the army. Then I figured he needed me more than you did. Where is Andrew right now, do you know?"

"I don't know. He wouldn't say."

"What if he came here?"

"He could have, I suppose. He likes to go deep-sea fishing. He misses that."

"So he could be in one of those boats out there."

He points to the dots of fishing boats, their rails lined by men with faces too far off to identify.

"Not likely. Michael? Be careful not to take on too much of Walter's bitterness."

"Why would you say that?"

"You were such an easygoing young man when I met you. So relaxed. I'd hate to see you lose that. Walter's gone, we can't change that. Michael's here. He has a life, right now. I wouldn't want to see you waste too much of it in anger. You don't have to pick up his bad habits, either," she says, indicating the cigarette.

He turns on her, knowing his reaction is wrong, knowing it's just the opposite of what she's asking him to do. Knowing he is proving her point.

He feels the hardness set into his face.

"I don't think you have the right to advise me. Because you have no idea how this feels."

"No, that's true. I don't."

"Don't ever tell me that what I'm feeling is wrong. I have a right to his feelings."

"Okay," she says. "My mistake."

CHAPTER TWENTY-SIX

Andrew

Andrew stands at the rail of the boat, legs wide set to resist the pitch and roll, and casts his line again.

He turns a heavy gaze to the boardwalk, and locates the approximate spot where they stood on the night he proposed to Mary Ann. It's part of why he came back to this place. A good day of fishing is an easy thing to point to as his motivation, but that spot on the boardwalk, that means something. That's something he's missed.

Several couples line the boardwalk rail, too far away to really see.

He wonders if they know they stand on sacred ground. He

wonders if they know enough to respect it. He figures they probably don't.

His eyes feel heavy, grainy. His neck seems to surrender too easily to gravity. He hasn't slept well for days. It's catching up with him.

Half asleep, he feels a sharp jerk on the pole in his hands, thinks he has a bite. He opens his eyes to see the man beside him grasping the rod tightly.

"Almost lost your rod, mister. What'd you do, take some seasick pills?"

Andrew steps into the narrow galley to sit, to lean back, to rest his tired eyes.

He's just tired. He just hasn't been able to get any sleep. It's the dreams. He's never been seasick a day in his life. It was Walter who puked his guts out all the way from San Diego to Guadalcanal. Andrew always felt fine.

No sooner does he lean back on the bench than he dreams his eyes are still open, dreams that he is awake on this bench in the galley of this boat, and Walter comes to sit down beside him.

He wears white ducks, a white short-sleeved shirt, smokes a Lucky. His hair is neatly oiled back.

"No, please," Andrew says, thinking it sounds weak, but not knowing how to change that. "No more dreams. I can't take any more dreams. What do I have to do to make them stop?"

Walter says, "Be a big, brave guy. Go see the man again."

"Steeb?"

"The very one."

"And say what?"

"You'll know."

"Okay, here's a question for you," Andrew says. "If this Steeb guy knows so much, why does he think Mrs. Mac-Gurdy's cat was named Angel?"

"Because she was."

"No, her name was Henrietta."

"Wrong again, old man. Angel, like me."

"You couldn't remember shit when you were alive, why should I take your word for it?"

Walter grins, crushes the butt of his cigarette under his heel.

"Hey. Andrew. Have I ever lied to you before, that you know of?"

He puts his hand on Andrew's shoulder, shakes him awake.

Andrew opens his eyes to see a deckhand shaking him.

"We're back in dock, sir."

"Oh. Oh, of course."

As he joins the line moving to the rear of the boat to disembark, he thinks he sees Mary Ann on the boardwalk. But he's just a little too far away to know for sure. Walking arm in arm with her is a young man who looks a lot like Michael Steeb.

He blinks hard, shakes the sleep out of his brain. When he looks up again, they're gone, blended into the crowd. Or, more likely, they were never there at all.

Great, he thinks, now I'm hallucinating.

He knows he needs sleep.

He knows he can't hold out much longer.

· ★ ·

Back in his motel room, about eight o'clock at night, Andrew wades through the jungle in his dream.

Walter walks in line behind him.

"Whit!" Walter shouts suddenly. "Croc!"

And he throws his body up against Andrew's.

Andrew jumps, turns with his rifle ready, and Walter laughs. The other guys in the outfit laugh.

Andrew just stands there in the mud, grasping his rifle, feeling his heartbeat settle again. Listening to the guys laugh at him. He thinks he can feel his face redden. He really doesn't think it's funny to trick a guy into thinking he's about to be eaten by a crocodile. Of all the guys in this stinking outfit, he least expected it from Walter.

"Whatsa matter, Whit," Oscar says, "can't take a joke?"

Depends on the joke, he thinks. But he decides to walk on, let it go by. What choice does he have, really? But it stays with him, a hard, pointed little grudge wedged above his diaphragm, like a chunk of bad food that just won't digest.

Coming from Walter, he figures it isn't going to be forgotten anytime soon.

After a slow, bad mile or so, they stumble up onto dry land and hear the first shots. Unexpected shots. On the very day they were expecting no combat situations, suddenly the outfit is pinned down by enemy fire. Ambushed by an enemy they were sure had left the island.

Andrew turns to see the Browning aimed at Walter's head.

The bullet flies.

"Wait!" Walter says, and holds up his hand. The bullet stops halfway to its destination, frozen in the air.

He turns to Andrew and smiles. It's an eerie, unnatural smile. "Push me out of the way," he says.

The bullet waits.

"What?"

"You're right there, Andrew. Push me out of the way."

"I—"

"Fivefourthreetwoone. Too late."

The bullet comes free again, and a shower of blood and bone sprays in Andrew's direction. He drops to his belly.

"Oops. Good reflexes," Walter says. He's lying on his back in the mud. His head is shattered, nearly half of it is missing, but his lips still move. He's still looking at Andrew and talking to him. "Where were those great reflexes a second ago?"

Andrew screams, pulling at the hair on the sides of his head.

"I can't stand it anymore. I can't take any more of this. What do I have to do to make it stop?"

"I told you, buddy."

"And if I go see him? Then this will stop?"

"It'll stop as soon as you make the decision."

"Okay. I'll go."

Walter sits up, then pulls to his feet. His head has been restored to its original condition. He is whole and alive.

"Good choice, buddy," he says.

He shakes Andrew's hand.

· ★ ·

For almost three days, Andrew stays in his motel room and catches up on his sleep. He gets up from time to time to eat, smoke a cigarette, go to the bathroom.

He decides it was all a trick played by his own mind, but it's over. Stress, nothing more. All in the past.

He decides it's not really necessary to go see Steeb.

The next time he falls asleep, he dreams he's in the gym at the old high school, working out with the wrestling team. He can't see the man poised behind him.

He's taken down immediately, and the whistle blows, but he's not allowed to get up. His arm remains pinned, and he bears the full weight of the man who defeated him.

"Get the hell off me," he says. "It's over."

He hears Walter's voice in his ear.

"Don't welsh on me, buddy. You renege, I renege."

He wakes up, wipes sweat off his forehead.

"Okay!" he shouts to the empty room. "Okay, I'll go."

CHAPTER TWENTY-SEVEN

Walter

Okay.

Now, as the man says, we're getting somewhere.

Now I honestly believe that life and I have broken Andrew down to the point where he really will go, and he really will listen. Not well, but he'll try. It's a start. He's got a truckload of stubborn left to get in our way, but at least it's a start.

I can only hope you haven't lost whatever measure of respect you might've had for me because of my tactics.

Put yourself in my place. I mean, when you're dead, if you can't come through in somebody's dream, what's left to you? It's definitely too late to say it with flowers.

I don't normally antagonize Andrew, or even allow any-body else to antagonize him, for that matter. I was usually the one to insist he be treated well.

There're only two exceptions I can think of. One is an un-pleasant thing I said to him one night in camp, and then a good bit later there was the second, the little joke I played on him about the croc. But he's forgotten that. At least he had until the dream, and even so, he might think that part never happened.

It was unlike me, that's the thing. I'm not a big teaser. Never was.

It's just that it was starting to get to me. I was beginning to feel like he didn't even want me around anymore. I'd try to be his friend, half the time he'd try to be mine, then he'd be at my throat again. No reason I could see except that something re-minded him of Mary Ann.

I'm not a blind man. I know what love does to a guy, even if it doesn't do it to me.

So far as I know, those were the only times I ever let out a little aggression.

I was hurt.

Imagine putting a woman before our friendship like that. If that's what love does, you can have it. Know what I mean?

And as far as the little croc incident, he forgot it right away. Because not fifteen minutes later, it all came down. So which part of the day are you more likely to remember? My buddy got his head blown off, or he tricked me into thinking he was a crocodile?

That's one way to lose a resentment, fast. Some of our most telling actions get swept under the carpet because life just steamrolls on. And if you're like me, more often than not, you like it that way. In some ways, I'm almost glad it ended there, before things got ugly. Much as I loved Andrew, good friends as we were, there was a real potential for things to get ugly.

Let me give you an example of what I mean. That little unpleasant incident I referred to earlier.

Let me tell you where I am.

We're in camp, a couple of miles from the mountain. It's dusk, and we're just finishing up eating. Me and Andrew, we're sitting with Jay, talking about food. Real food. Like we haven't seen for a while.

We're the three musketeers. Bobby is already gone.

Then Jay starts talking about his girlfriend. He talks about her a lot. He particularly likes to talk about her around us, because we listen. Unlike the other guys, we don't interrupt with stories of our girlfriends. I don't like to talk about Mary Ann all that much. Andrew would love to talk about her, but, you know. It's a thorny situation.

After a while I get up, and I walk down to the river to wash out my mess kit. While I do, I look over my shoulder, I'm not sure why.

Andrew is pulling something out of the lining of his helmet and showing it to Jay. That's where the guys usually keep important photos. Their mom or their girl. Usually their girl. Once or twice before I noticed that Andrew had something in his helmet, but he never talks about it to me. If he's got a picture of his mom in there, why the big secret?

So I go back, and I pick up Andrew's helmet off the ground, and I help myself.

Damned if it's not a picture of Mary Ann. Cut from the

high school yearbook. To make matters worse, it's not her class picture. It's one of the pictures from the prom. Mary Ann is wearing the wrist corsage I gave her. Here's the bad part: I was in that picture, too. He cut me out with a scissors. I can just see a little bit of my hand on her arm.

I look up, and Andrew is on his feet, facing me. There are a lot of ways he could play this moment. He could be contrite or act like it's no big deal. But no, that's not Andrew, is it? He wants to fight me. He's standing in front of me like he had her a minute ago, and I just stole her away, and he's willing to punch my lights out to get her back.

Only trouble is, she's home safe, stateside. This is just a scrap of paper. But he looks ready to fight.

And me? I'm pretty peeved. I've just about had enough of this. I knew we had a situation here, but this is just getting way out of hand.

"Wow, Andrew," I say. "That really is a pretty girl you carry around in your hat, there, buddy. Only one problem."

"Yeah, well, somebody had to care about her that much." He's not quite yelling, but guys are turning to look. "Somebody had to care enough to carry her picture off to war." He turns to look at Jay. Jay is on his feet now, in case we really are about to come to blows. Andrew tells Jay, and pretty much the rest of the unit, "Walter has a lovely picture of a lemon pie in his helmet. You should ask to see it sometime."

Then nobody says anything for a minute, and I realize that the camp is quiet. The whole unit is quiet. Listening.

"Andrew," I tell him, "you can say anything you want to try to make me sound like a pathetic loser, but I'm not the one carrying around a picture of somebody else's girl."

Not a very nice thing to say, you're probably thinking. You're right. It's not. But I'm a young, live human right now. If pushed, I'm just as likely as anybody to push back.

Then, to add injury to insult, I keep the picture of Mary Ann. Put it away in the breast pocket of my uniform.

That's too much for Andrew. That's what breaks him. He comes charging at me, but Jay gets hold of him and won't let go. He's saying soothing things in Andrew's ear, but he's holding damn tight, and every now and then Andrew is bucking like he still wants to get at me.

Jay says, "Hey, buddy. Hey. We got enough enemies here. We got Germany and Japan and Italy, we start fighting each other, then where will we be?"

Andrew nods, and Jay cuts him loose. He just walks away.

Jay walks over and slaps me on the arm. "Whoa, I thought you guys were best buddies."

I say, "Yeah. So did I."

"Well, I guess it doesn't help that he's in love with your girl."

There. See how easy that is to say? You would think anybody could do it. You would think somebody besides Jay would have set that on the table by now.

I don't see Andrew again that night. I see him in the morning, and we just go on like nothing ever happened. We just take right up from there.

But a little bit of the feeling stays. We watch each other a little more carefully after that. Hold things a little closer to our chests.

Jay dies in the morning, run through with that bayonet I was so sure had gotten Andrew. I take that mortar round with

Mary Ann's picture in my breast pocket, and it survives in surprisingly good condition. A little pockmarked and battered but more or less in one piece.

I never give it back to Andrew. A few weeks later I die with it in my breast pocket. It gets sorted and boxed with some other personal effects and shipped back to Ocean City along with what's left of my body.

If that's winning, it's not all it's cracked up to be.

CHAPTER TWENTY-EIGHT

Michael

They stop at a florist downtown, buy a mixed bouquet. Take it with them on a long bus ride. It's a half-mile walk from the bus stop to the cemetery.

They walk slowly, like lovers with nowhere special to go.

The flowers dangle from Michael's hand. They come through the gate, past neatly tended rows of graves.

"Over there?" he asks. "With the servicemen?"

"Yes. It's that second row."

He puts his arm around her shoulders, she slides hers around his waist. He squeezes her tightly and kisses her on the temple. She smiles.

Isn't this simple? he thinks. Isn't this calm? Why couldn't we be this calm before? He got them both high before the ride over. He figures that must be the secret.

Then they find what he's come here looking for.

"Oh, whoa," he says when he sees it. His stomach drops away like the big ride on the roller coaster. He had allowed himself to relax. He hadn't expected a big reaction. "Whoa, that's really weird."

"Anything you can describe?"

"Hell, no. Wow."

"Maybe you should sit down."

He sinks to his knees on the grass in front of it, flowers scraping the ground.

"'Walter M. Crowley. 1921 to 1942.' Mathew? After my father?"

"Very good."

"Where is my father? Is he gone?"

"Yes, many years."

"Oh."

He feels her come down to her knees behind him, feels her chin on his shoulder. He reaches back for her hands and pulls them around his waist.

"I used to come here every year, before we moved. On your birthday." She kisses a spot behind his ear. "Go ahead, put the flowers down."

"No, you do it. It feels too weird."

She leans them both forward and sets the flowers in front of the marker.

"I used to talk to you. Every time I came."

"What'd you say?"

"Just caught you up on what had been happening since you were gone. Told you I loved you. That sort of thing."

"What *has* been happening since I was gone?" His father died, for one, and he never thought to ask about that. What else hasn't he wondered about?

He hears and feels her breathing turn shallow.

"Some good, some bad."

"For example."

"Come here," she says.

They both stand and then walk, holding hands, to a far corner of the cemetery. She leads him down a row, stops, turns.

He looks where she looks.

"'Kathryn Elizabeth Quinn,'" he reads out loud. "Who's that?" Before she can answer, he knows. "Oh, no. Not Katie. She was so young."

He doesn't so much mean that she would have been young if she'd lived. He hasn't done the math on that yet. Just that he's remembering her as he last saw her, and she's so young. Then again, Katie was never young. She skipped her childhood completely to go right on to something more complicated and troublesome.

"She would have been fifty-three."

"So why isn't she?"

"About five years ago, just before Andrew and I moved away, she . . . took her own life."

"Why?"

"Who ever knows why?"

"Well, tell me what you do know. She was married to this guy Quinn. What was he like?"

"Oh, you wouldn't have liked him. He ran around on her."

He waits quietly for a minute, listens to the silence. He senses an "and." He smells it, feels the weight of it between them.

"And . . ."

"And, we're not sure, but we think he might have hit her. She always denied it. But you know, there's only just so many times one person runs into a door or trips on the stairs."

He wonders if she feels his body stiffen, his arm tighten around her. She must.

"And where is this Quinn now?"

"Why would you want to know that, Michael?"

"Just answer the question."

"You know, this is what I meant about not getting too wrapped up in Walter's bitterness. It's over, Michael, just accept it. Everybody else has."

His arm comes away from her, his voice comes up loud enough to startle them both. "Get used to it? Get used to hearing that some asshole beat up my baby sister?"

An elderly couple three rows over turns to stare.

"It's over, Michael. You can't help her now."

"I don't want to hear it, Mary Ann. I don't want to hear that shit from you. I haven't had all this adjustment time, like you have. I had forty years stolen. Would you have accepted it, just like that, a minute after you found out?"

As he shouts at her, a detached voice in his head says, So this is what it feels like to lose your temper.

"No, of course not," she says. "I'm sorry." And he sees she's crying.

Oh God, he thinks. Now I went and made her cry.

He grabs her, holds her close.

"I'm sorry. I didn't mean to yell at you. You're the last person in the world I want to yell at. I'm sorry."

Before she can answer, he kisses her. On the mouth. Long and deep. Not the way you kiss your grandmother.

She allows it for a handful of seconds, then pushes him away with her hands on his chest.

"They're staring at us." She motions with her head to the old couple.

"I don't care."

"*I* care," she says, as if she owes him an apology.

He steps back, turns, walks across the cemetery to Walter's grave. He doesn't look around to see if she walks with him.

He picks up the bouquet of flowers, then turns back to see her standing where he left her, watching.

He carries the flowers back and sets them on Katie's grave.

"So long, little sister," he says. "Sorry I wasn't around to help. Not that I was much help when I was around."

He realizes he has to get brave now. He has to find out about Robbie. Even in the middle of the shock of this. He still has to know.

"How's Robbie? How's my kid brother?"

"He's fine. He's an investment broker in Dallas. He sends us a card every Christmas."

"Okay, good."

"Your 'kid brother' is fifty-five."

"Oh, shit," he says, head in hands. "Oh, wow."

· ★ ·

Mary Ann's flight leaves first.

He stands at the gate with her, long after the boarding call is announced.

He hugs her more often, and for greater duration, than should be necessary to say good-bye for now.

At least, he hopes it's just for now.

"I miss you already," he says. "I wish you'd let us be a little closer."

"Don't push, Michael. Please. I'm not strong enough for both of us. Just because it happened once—"

"Twice."

"Okay, twice."

"Once at the old mine, once in my bed that night."

"Okay, you're right, twice."

"I remember the second time very well. You yelled out my name."

"Did I really?"

"Yeah, you really did." He smiles at her now, and it makes her blush.

"Which name was that?"

"Walter."

"I'm sorry."

He shrugs. "Sounded okay to me."

He pulls her in close again. "I love you." He delivers it directly into her ear.

She draws back, holds him by both shoulders. "I'm going to ask you a tough question, Michael. You'll hate it. You'll probably hate me for asking it."

"I doubt that."

"Why couldn't you have loved me this much back then?"

Michael feels as though the wind has been knocked out of him, or as though he's run a mile uphill. It takes time to re-group.

"Well, you're half right," he says. "I hate the question."

He's relieved when she boards without demanding an answer.

He stands at the window long after her plane shrinks to a pinpoint and disappears.

CHAPTER TWENTY-NINE

Walter

Two times I remember with my kid brother, Robbie. I don't know if they have anything to do with each other. I guess on a feeling level they do.

This first place I am, Andrew and I are walking down to the high school on a Saturday morning because we have a meet. It's nearly summer and already feeling hot. It's going to be hard, running in this heat.

We could take the bus, but the bus is hot, and we don't really like it. It's a good warm-up, walking.

Andrew says, "Don't look now." Motions with his chin, back over his shoulder.

I turn around to look. Robbie is following us, about thirty paces behind. When he sees me look, he stops dead. Looks up at the sky. Then I start walking again. I turn around, and he's started walking again, too. When I look back, of course he stops.

It's all just too entirely stupid.

So I say, "If you want to walk with us, kid, just get up here and walk with us."

Andrew hits me on the arm. Hard. Maybe harder than he meant to.

"Ow. What's that for?"

"Don't tell him that."

"Why not?"

"Because he might do it."

He doesn't, though. He acts like he didn't hear. I give up, and we walk to school like that, Robbie following thirty paces behind.

He sits all the way at the top of the bleachers while we warm up.

Then my first race comes up, and I don't see him, or maybe I've forgotten to look. It's such a great moment for me. I think I block everything else out.

I'm in the starting position, waiting for the gun. I love that position. Something about having my body stretched out like that, waiting to spring. It makes me feel like some beautiful, fast animal, like a cheetah. Then my body hears and feels the gun. I'm running.

It's all in the heart, running. Not to brag on myself, but I have the heart for this. I mean that in two completely different ways. Physically, your heart needs to be big and strong, ready to pump buckets when you really need it. But there's another kind of heart. It takes courage to run that hard. It takes me having more heart than the guy behind me. If he's starting to catch up, I have to open my heart more, run on sheer emotion. The body falls into the background here. Turns into a machine. My legs go like pistons in a combustion engine. You don't think about your engine turning as you drive, right? It just keeps running.

I always win on heart.

This is not to say that someday I might not have found somebody who ran the same way, and right at the finish line, learned that his heart was just a little bigger. I'm not saying it couldn't have happened. I'm just saying it didn't.

As I come down the stretch to the finish, there's Robbie. In the lowest, closest bleacher. Right at the finish line. Right there, where he could almost reach out and touch me as I go by, right at the moment I win.

I decide I have to let him know I know he's there. Or really, that I care. So I give him a little salute. Just two fingers, touching my forehead. I never did it before, but the meaning is clear, I think. Just a little, "Hi, kid."

I hit the tape and try to come down, and as I do, I look over my shoulder, and he's saluting me back.

He's not a born athlete, Robbie, but he's living his life through me. I decide if he ever comes to a meet again, I'll do it again. It has the feel of something that deserves to be a tradition.

I run one more, and win that, too. And give Robbie another salute.

Andrew competes in the pole vault, but he has a bad day.

Knocks down the cross bar and lands badly, stoves his shoulder. Not enough to go to the hospital, but he's rubbing it all the way home. Maybe it is bad enough to go to the hospital. With him, you'd never know. But what would they do about an injury like that, anyway? It just has to hurt like hell for a while.

"Put some liniment on that," I say while we're walking home.

"Yeah, whatever," he says. He doesn't want to be hurt, and talking about it doesn't help.

I turn around, and there's Robbie. Thirty paces behind.

See, I thought we'd had some sort of breakthrough. I figured he'd walk home with us like one of the boys.

I motion to him. Come on.

He looks up at the sky like he doesn't see.

When we get home, my mom's made cookies. Oatmeal with chocolate chips.

"What did you boys do today?" she asks.

I thought she knew I had a meet, but maybe not. Or maybe she's just doing that thing where she doesn't want to put words in my mouth.

"We both went to my track meet," I say.

Robbie is stuffing two cookies in his mouth at once, so I'll have to do all the talking.

"Well, that's nice," she says. "I like it when you boys do things together."

The sad part is, for me and Robbie, that really was together. That was one of our best days.

Now it's a couple of years later, after I've already gotten my orders but before I ship out.

I'm walking into my dad's hardware store. Showing up for my regular shift.

Robbie's there, in one of those leather aprons Dad wears, and makes me wear, when we're manning the store. This is a new one for Robbie, though. He does the stock room sometimes, but today Dad is teaching him to run the paint mixer. This is genuine training.

They both look at me like I'm from another planet.

"Walter," my dad says. "What are you doing here?"

"I work here."

"Not now, you don't. You got your orders."

"Yeah, but I'm here. I mean, I haven't shipped out yet." We never discuss things. The most important moments of our lives are supposed to go without saying.

"You might be gone a long time," my dad says. "You need this time. This is your time. Use it to get your affairs in order."

Robbie is silent for all this, just staring.

I say, "Jeez, Dad. Isn't that what they say to people who are about to die?"

Bad thing to say. We all just stare at each other, and I can see in their eyes that I should have kept quiet. I feel like a comedian dying onstage.

"Take your girl out," Dad says, covering over the moment. "Take her to dinner and buy her flowers if you can afford it. If that's too much money, take her walking on the beach. She'll be alone a long time. That's a hard time for a girl."

"Okay, Dad."

I turn and walk out of the store. As I do, I'm hit with this moment of real elation, because I don't have to sell hardware anymore.

"Walter!"

I turn back, and there's Robbie, standing on the sidewalk, yelling at me.

"You weren't ever supposed to say things like that!"

He's standing with his legs wide apart, the way he does when he's feeling challenged. Like he wants to make sure the world can't knock him over. He's standing under the sign that says CROWLEY AND SONS HARDWARE. That living, breathing, paint-and-wood proof that something has to give. He looks so grown-up in that leather apron. He looks like a man. A hardware man.

I think, God help you, Robbie, you are the next man of the family now, the new heir.

"Sorry," I say.

Under my breath I wish him luck.

CHAPTER THIRTY

Michael

He steps up onto his own porch like he's never seen it before, or only seen it in a dream. Dennis sticks his head out the door, looks him over, and his face changes.

Don't even say it, Michael thinks.

"You've changed, man."

"I know."

"You look about ten years older."

"Try forty."

"You got a letter from Andrew."

"I did? Where?"

"On the kitchen table. It's been there for days."

He runs inside, rummages through the mail, pulls it free. It's written on stationery from a hotel in Ocean City. His heart misses for a split second, wondering if Andrew was there the whole time.

5 / 18 / 82

Dear Mr. Steeb,

After careful consideration I see that you're right. We must at least talk.

I'm flying in on the 2nd, flight 292 from New Jersey. If you can meet me around 4:15, great. If not, I can get there on my own steam, like last time.

If there's a problem with that, please let me know immediately.

Sincerely,

Andrew Whittaker

He reads it twice, then lays it face up on the table. He sees Dennis watching him.

"Dennis, what day is this?"

"I think it's the second."

"Yeah, I had a funny feeling that's what you were going to say."

· ★ ·

He arrives at the airport nearly twenty-five minutes early, calls Mary Ann first thing.

Her phone rings four, five, six times. A coldness creeps out from a deep part of him. She's not going to answer.

Answer. Please answer.

She picks up the phone.

"Hi," he says. "It's me. Were you napping or something?"

"No, I was just out in the garden."

"I know where Andrew is."

"You do? Where?"

"On his way to my house."

"Well, thank you for telling me. I've been worried. How did he sound?"

"I don't know. He just wrote me a note." He stares out past the pay phone, through the window, sees a plane depart, shrink almost to disappearing. He feels a sharp pain in his gut, as if he's talking to her and letting her go at the same time. "You know what I forgot to tell you? Thanks for taking me to see Mom. She's going to die soon. Really soon. If she hasn't already. I sure would have hated to miss seeing her. I got so wrapped up in us, I forgot to tell you how much it meant."

"I understand."

"Tell me I'll see you again."

"I think you will."

"I'm scared, Mary Ann." He listens to her silence, pretends he can hear her breathing, pretends it's enough breath to support his own life as well, so it can't be lost. "This is so important."

"It's tearing you apart, isn't it?"

He shifts suddenly, can't find it in himself to be serious another second.

"Well, you know me. I'm like one of my ratty old bikes. You want to rebuild me, you got to tear me down first."

"You can call if you need me."

"I know." He hears tears quaver behind his voice, wonders if she does, too. Wonders if the tears go deep enough to travel the miles that stand between them. If only that were all. "Thanks."

· ★ ·

As Andrew steps into the terminal, Michael holds out his hand, and they exchange a firm shake.

Andrew's eyes are less direct. He glances briefly at Michael, a sidelong glance.

"You got your hair cut."

"Yeah."

They retrieve his luggage in silence, carry it to the van in more silence.

"I didn't come here voluntarily," Andrew says.

"I know why you came here."

"Do you really? I don't."

Michael lets him in the driver's side, cranks the engine.

"You came here so the dreams would stop."

Andrew whips his head in Michael's direction, then stares out the window again.

"What do you know about the dreams?"

"Andrew," he says, and pulls out onto the highway, "why exactly do you think I drove eighteen hundred miles round trip to stand at your door for forty-five seconds and make an ass of myself? Did you assume it was a hobby?"

"I didn't know what to assume."

"I wanted the nightmares to stop."

"Did they?"

"Oh, yes, cleared up fine. I sleep like a baby now. How 'bout you? You wrote a few days ago to say you were coming. How've you slept since then?"

"Fine," he says in a faraway voice, as though he's not hearing himself talk. "I've been sleeping fine."

"So, are you going to stay for a couple of days?"

"I don't know. You only stayed forty-five seconds."

"But we weren't done, were we? We just set it in motion."

"Okay, I'll stay until we're done. How do we know when we're done?"

Michael flashes Andrew a smile, and Andrew turns in time to take it in. It's not a smile brimming with confidence, but it will have to do.

"We'll know."

"Yes," Andrew says, "so I hear."

CHAPTER THIRTY-ONE

Andrew

He sits with the young man on the bank of a creek, the flow of water over rocks like background music. He props himself on the slope, knees up, elbows dug into the soft dirt.

The cover of scrub oaks provides a pleasing dapple of sun and shade.

Steeb says, "I wish we wouldn't always boil this down to me defending my position."

"Well, next time don't adopt such an indefensible position."

He watches Steeb pick up a small rock and toss it to the opposite bank.

"I didn't adopt this position," he says. "It adopted me. Oh! I got a real good one." His excitement is evident in his voice, and it worries Andrew. So far, his worst fear is that Steeb will remember something irrefutable. "Okay. I'm in the hospital. And believe me when I tell you it won't be over until you know how I got there. But for now, the magazine."

"What magazine?"

"Allow me to jog your memory. You traded a whole carton of cigarettes for it."

"So? Anybody could have told you about the magazine."

"I had to keep it a secret. Otherwise the orderlies would have stolen it. Only ones who knew were you, me, and Billy Ray."

"Who's Billy Ray?"

"That Texan in the next bed."

"Oh, yeah. Then Billy Ray told you."

"He never made it out of that hospital, remember? He died three days before I was released."

"Oh, yeah. I forgot. But who knows who he told, anyway? Or who Walter told, for that matter."

He looks to Steeb's face. He looks into his eyes, then down at the creek again. Watches the water as it winds, cuts paths. He can't look at those eyes. The scorn is too much like Walter's scorn. It cuts paths. Slowly, like water on stone, but over the years it wears you down.

"Andrew, you're impossible. No matter what I tell you, you say Walter must have told somebody who told me. Who was he telling these minute life details to, anyway? Who was this magic person who knew every movement, but who we never met?"

"Makes more sense than your explanation."

"You're impossible."

Then Steeb falls silent, strangely, conspicuously silent, and Andrew feels he can hear him think. He reads grounds for fear into the silence, and his stomach tightens, prepared for what will come next.

"Okay, here goes. When you got sent home from the war, you called my mom . . ." Andrew misses the next couple of lines, his brain caught in the last one. When he got home from the war? Walter was dead by then. How can this string of information go on without him? " . . . and when you got to our house, you stopped in the front yard, and you just stood there, staring at the house, and then you dropped down to your knees—well, knee—and nearly started crying. And this I would say was quite a sacrifice, because you'd screwed your knee all up in that injury on Papua—"

"Wait, wait, wait. This is all after Walter was dead."

"I was there, though. You didn't see me, but I was there. And then Mom came out and got down with you and put her arms around you, and told you not to cry, which you weren't exactly, and then she started crying, too."

"Millie could have told you that."

"But not what you saw that brought you to your knees. Because she was in the kitchen, making that pie that should have been for me. She didn't even know you were there yet."

"So, what did I see?"

"That gold star in the window. The symbol for a lost son. It broke you down."

"Lucky guess," he says, but he hears the waver in his voice, and he can't pretend Steeb didn't hear it, too.

"You didn't know I was there, but guess who did? Nicky did, that's who. Remember what he was doing? Running around and around on the front lawn, jumping at nothing? Mom said he was happy to see you, but he wasn't looking at you. Was he?" Andrew avoids Steeb's face as the young man waits for his answer. "Was he, Andrew? And then you went inside and ate two pieces of lemon pie, one for me. Damn, I wanted to eat that for myself, too."

"I know, it's all you could ever talk about."

Then he hears what he said.

Steeb is nice enough not to point it out.

It appears that the conversation is over for now.

· ★ ·

Steeb gets it in his head that they should go deep-sea fishing, because, he says, it would be, "Just like old times."

"Using what for a boat?"

"Dennis has a boat."

Andrew wants to see this boat first, to judge for himself that it's seaworthy.

Steeb takes him up a winding driveway to a building that he would classify as a workshop of sorts. Obviously someone has taken its construction seriously, put more energy into it than into the house.

A young man with a ratlike face is working on a bicycle in the corner. Andrew mistrusts him almost as much as he mistrusts his host. But the boat is a beauty. A little Woodson skiff, twelve feet, with its own trailer. No motor that he can see, but good name, good construction.

"Hey, this is a nice boat."

"Yeah, Dennis traded a Harley for it, but now he never uses it. Oh. Andrew, this is Dennis. Dennis, Andrew."

Dennis wipes his hands on a shop towel and shakes.

"So you're Andrew. Man, I've heard a lot about you."

Andrew chooses not to react. He just says, "This is too nice a boat to have and not use."

"You want it, man? I'll let it go cheap."

"I live in Albuquerque."

"Oh. Sorry, man. Forget I mentioned it."

Steeb asks if they can take the boat out, and Dennis says sure. He says, "Take the truck, too, it'll pull the bumper right off your piece-of-shit van."

So Steeb backs the old Chevy step-side pickup to the shop door, and Dennis and Andrew hitch the boat up to go. Suddenly Andrew feels full of reservations.

"What, no motor?"

"Andrew. We never had a motor way back when. We rowed."

"I was younger."

"I'll row."

"Fishing rods?"

"We can rent them at the pier."

He starts to say bait, tackle, but knows if the pier rents rods, it will have all that, too.

No, there's only one real reservation, and it's one he won't share.

What's to stop this young man from hitting him in the head with an oar and dropping him into the deep? He could say it was an accident.

Is this really how he has to die? Is that the force that brought him here against his will?

In the end, he goes along anyway.

He feels he's lost the option to base decisions on such trivia as survival.

CHAPTER THIRTY-TWO

Walter

Here's where I am.

It's Wednesday night. My last Wednesday night as a civilian. I've just been cut loose from the hardware store. I'm standing on Mary Ann's front porch with flowers behind my back.

It's still light, but getting dusky. I love this time of day. The next-door neighbor's dog is barking at me, and I'm saying, "It's only me, Bruno. You know me, boy. Calm down."

It's still the end of winter, but the weather's been nice. Mid-fifties. It almost feels like spring.

Mary Ann's mother answers the door. She smiles when she sees I'm hiding something. She seems to get the picture. Mary Ann's mother likes me so much it almost scares me. It makes me feel like no matter how good a person I manage to be, the truth of me will never measure up.

She calls Mary Ann down from upstairs, and then goes back to clearing the table. Cleaning up the dishes from dinner.

Mary Ann's face lights up when she sees me.

"Walter. What are you doing here? Don't you have to work?"

"Nope."

"But the store is open till eight on Wednesdays."

"Not my problem. I have the night off."

I have my life off, really. So far I can only relate to this one Wednesday night.

She comes galloping down the stairs, and I take the flowers out from behind my back. We stand at the bottom of the stairs with our foreheads touching, looking down at them.

"How sweet," she says.

"My dad said I should take you out to dinner and buy you flowers, or just take you for a walk on the beach if I couldn't afford all that."

"I knew there was something I liked about your dad."

I almost say, Great, you want him? But the mood is just right, and I don't want to kill it. Besides, you don't really say things like that out loud.

"Thing is," I say, "the truth is somewhere in between. So how about flowers and a walk on the beach?"

"I'll get my coat," she says.

· ★ ·

We're walking along the boardwalk together. As slowly as we can walk. Like we're afraid to get where we're going too fast, which is funny, because we're not going anywhere.

I've just finished telling her about this dance on Friday night, which I figure I can just barely afford. I don't tell her I can only just barely afford it. I just say, Let's go. It seems like it'll be a good last hurrah, because Andrew's and my train leaves Monday morning.

She tells me she got Monday morning off work, so she can see me off at the station.

"Mrs. Blanton gave you the morning off?"

"I know. Isn't that amazing?"

Mary Ann works at the five-and-dime, and the owner is really strict.

She says, "I don't think it's about me, so much. I think it's about the war effort."

That makes a degree of sense. Everybody is careful these days to maintain just the right attitude toward the war effort. I guess seeing your young man off at the station has been elevated to the most noble and patriotic thing a woman can do. Unless, of course, you're giving the war effort your son.

You're probably thinking I'm going to tell you I'm scared to death right now, that I can feel the weight of the war like a sword hanging over my head. Not even close. I'm just floating along in this state of elation because all of life's normal responsibilities and irritations are gone.

It's like a sheet of blue-lined paper, the kind you write on at school, but with the lines suddenly missing. No structure.

Nothing is predictable. Everything that might happen now is new.

Sometimes disasters make me feel that way. When my Uncle Frank died, they came and took me out of school. It was an unhappy thing, but there was something exciting in knowing that all the drudging, repetitious parts of life had been put on hold. Except then it was just a day or two. Now my life is an unmarked page for as far as I can see.

I hope that doesn't make me sound abnormal.

Anyway, we walk down onto the beach after a while. Take off our shoes and tie them together and hang them over our shoulders. I roll my pant legs a couple of turns, and we walk right at the edge of the water. Even though it's cold.

Every now and then a wave comes in a little bigger and harder, and Mary Ann screams and runs and holds her skirt a little higher, and I laugh.

"What do you think about kids?" she asks.

"I like them in general. Why?"

"I think you'd be a good father."

"Do you?"

I'm not a very good older brother, but maybe it's not the same thing.

"Definitely. I want to have lots of kids," she says.

"Define lots."

"Four or five."

"That's lots."

Another big wave, and we have to run a few steps to duck it.

"Does that seem like a lot to you?" she asks. "How many

do you want?" Then she gets a little embarrassed and says, "I didn't mean . . . I mean . . . I wasn't trying to pressure you."

"It's okay," I say, and put an arm around her shoulders. "We're just talking. I'm thinking more like one or two, because it seems like when you have more than that, somebody always gets lost."

"Really?"

"Seems so to me."

"I guess I wouldn't know. Being an only child and all."

We stop walking, and I kiss her on the lips. And a big wave comes in and splashes her skirt and my pant legs, and then we're really cold. We're insane to be out here in our bare feet anyway. It's barely March. But we pretend it's not a problem.

I'm guessing this little idyllic scene is not what you were expecting. Maybe it seems different from what I've been describing up until now. Because I guess from the outside it all just seems so . . . Well, you know. Perfect.

But see, actually, this is what I've been trying to tell you. On the outside it was about as close as real life gets to perfect.

Maybe on the outside anything can be.

But really, we were great friends. Perfect friends. I couldn't have enjoyed her company more. Well, I guess I shouldn't put it that way. I should say that I couldn't have enjoyed her any more as a friend.

The only thing that really marred this lovely setup is that we were never going to get to the part about the kids, and some little place in me knew it.

It's that glimpse into the future that spoils the present. You know how people say, I wish I'd known then what I know now?

Not always such a good idea.

There's something to be said for not knowing squat.

Anyway, just so I don't make you too sick, I should tell you that things get a good bit less mushy after that.

We walk away from the water so we can't get surprised again, and we sit on the sand with our backs against one of the pilings. It's really dark now, and the stuff we talk about gets darker, too.

Like we talk about how often we'll write to each other, and how long we think it'll take for mail to get back and forth, and how long it might be before the war is over. If the war is ever over.

I start to lose that blank-paper elation and wish for my blue lines back. It's starting to dawn on me that in the long run my blue lines were better.

We're both shaking a little, because we're wet, but we're still pretending it doesn't matter. That we're not really cold. Because we don't want to have to go home and call this night over.

I'm looking at the stars and thinking that in just a few weeks I'll be on the other side of the world, and I wonder if the stars I'm looking at now will be the same stars I'll be looking at over there. If not, that's pretty terrifying. But really, I don't know.

And I know a little bit about astronomy, too. I've just never considered it from any angle but North America. I can figure we're all looking at the same stars in different seasons, but what stars I'll see when I get there, I don't know.

It feels like a strange thing not to know.

"What am I going to do without you?" she asks.

And you know, it doesn't change anything I've said before about Mary Ann and all those missing feelings, but right at the moment she feels like too much to lose.

CHAPTER THIRTY-THREE

Mary Ann

For the seventh night in a row, she sleeps in their bed alone. It's also the seventh night in thirty-eight years.

She is aware of the unused space, the noises she thinks she must hear every night and ignore.

She has been jumpy.

But tonight, she hears the bedsprings creak, independent of any movement on her part, and she's not afraid.

"I know that's you, Walter."

In a limited sense, she's been expecting him.

"I love that about you. I never could have pulled off any of this without you. You're my one willing participant."

"Yes," she says, rolling toward the voice, "I always was."

She wants to turn on a light but doesn't dare. The light of the moon and the streetlight are enough.

He sits on the edge of the bed in a dark suit and tie. He wears no tie bar, and when he leans in close, the tie dangles forward, and she reaches for it, strokes the silky material between her thumb and forefinger.

"Why can I feel this?" she says.

She feels swollen with emotion, almost overcome, but she knows to treat him like a bubble that might be easily broken.

"Maybe you're dreaming."

"I don't think so."

"Maybe you're dreaming that part." He stretches out beside her. Props up on one elbow and smiles. "What do you see when you look at me?"

"You're wearing that suit you wore on our last date. You look very well groomed. Why? Does that mean something?"

"Just that it's how you prefer to remember me. Because I don't look like anything, really." He reaches out and touches her hair, but she feels no physical sensation, only those that rise up from inside her, and she doesn't dare allow them much sway. "When I look at you I see red hair, and the most flawless skin."

"You're dreaming, dear."

He laughs, especially with his eyes. "I can't stay. I came to answer your question. Michael didn't answer because he doesn't know. I didn't even know. I had to borrow from that place that knows everything. You deserve an answer."

"I thought maybe you were gay."

"I asked myself that question, but I don't think so. I think I knew I was going to die. I didn't know I knew, but you know how it is."

She nods. She knows, more now than ever.

"It's like I was trying to chase you away. How can you let yourself love someone when it's almost time?"

"But you loved your family. And Andrew. And Nicky."

He shakes his head. He looks off toward the window and his eyes look deep somehow, like a well with no bottom.

"How do I explain the difference? It's like the difference between the past and the future. When you're growing up, you have a mom and dad, and a brother and sister, and a dog and a best friend. But you leave all that behind. Anyway. You're supposed to. They're not your future. They were going to lose you anyway."

"Walter. When I was with Michael, I mean close with him, was that really you?"

"Nothing's really me, sweetheart. That's as close as you'll get. This is as close as you'll get. It's not something we can restore."

He leans in to kiss her, and she gives with the feeling, meets him halfway, all the time knowing that hope will only set her up again.

She reaches for his face, but finds nothing.

When she opens her eyes again, she can still see him. She touches his hair. Nothing.

"I could feel your tie. Why can't I feel you?"

"Even dreams have limitations. I have to get back. I left those two floating in a boat in the Pacific Ocean. They might throw each other overboard without me."

"Wait."

"I can't."

"Just tell me if this is a dream."

"Yes and no, sweetheart."

"I have to tell you something."

But she knows she won't have time, because she doesn't know yet what it is. It might take the rest of her life to get the words just right.

"Don't," he says. "It'll only be taken away again. I'm not back. I'll never be back. I'm sorry. For everything."

She presses her eyes closed to fight the truth of the words. When she opens them again, she's awake. He's gone.

No, not gone. Never there.

He'll never be back.

Tears are good for you, she thinks, as hers take over.

She thanks God that Andrew is away. He's afraid of a simple thing like tears.

She wonders if she can let go of the whole forty years' worth before he comes home.

She gets off to a strong beginning.

CHAPTER THIRTY-FOUR

Michael

He rows until his arm muscles burn, but doesn't let that stop him. Andrew sits facing him, and now and then Michael glances at his face, gauging his level of concern.

He has no intention of asking what the problem is.

If Andrew has something to say, he's a big boy and should need no prompting.

As if reading that thought, Andrew says, "Why are we going so far out?"

"How far out do you think we should go?"

"No farther than I could row back."

"Why? Are you planning to throw me overboard?"

"I was just about to ask you the same question."

"Okay, Andrew, I'll answer the question honestly. I am quite purposefully rowing out farther than you could row back. I'm doing it because when the going gets tough, you'll try to bail on me. This way we don't go back until we resolve something."

"I don't like it. It makes me nervous."

Michael sets the oars and begins the process of tying a hook onto his line.

"That's because you're racked with guilt. You assume I must hate you. You're like guilt with legs. You built yourself on all that guilt, and now the guilt's killed the host organism and there's nothing left but guilt."

"What in God's name are you talking about?"

Michael notices that Andrew does not set up to fish. He must have forgotten why they pretended to come out here. Michael has forgotten, too, in one sense, but his hands go through the motions anyway. He ties a sinker onto the line.

"It wasn't my fault," Andrew says tightly. Michael waits, declines to match or raise him. "I didn't kill him." Already he raises his voice. Michael knows this would be Andrew's exit, if not for the precautions.

"No, but you helped."

"How dare you say that to me. I don't have to stay here and take this."

"Well, this time you do, actually."

Andrew looks around as if he might see options he'd over-looked.

"I did not help."

"You talked him into enlisting."

"He would have been drafted anyway."

"Yes, but by then he would have been married." He turns his eyes up from his work, watches Andrew's Adam's apple bob, watches his eyes. He feels oddly detached, as if reciting words by heart. As if Walter wasn't even here. "By the time Uncle Sam came for him, he would have married Mary Ann. Then it would be too late to break up the game plan."

"So you did bring me out here to kill me."

Michael laughs. "You're impossible, Andrew. What do I have to do to convince you that I love you?"

"Take me back to shore?"

"Not yet. Before we go back, you're going to admit that you wanted me to die, and I'm going to forgive you. Then I'm going to tell you some things that you'll find almost as bad, and you're going to forgive me."

He looks up to see Andrew's eyes, half shielded in armor, half scared, like a kid telling ghost stories.

Andrew lights a cigarette, and Michael notices it's filterless, notices the shaking of his hands.

"Those things'll kill you, Andrew."

"That's what I keep hoping, yes. Like Lucky Strikes are any better. What about food and water?"

"Why drag it out? If we get hungry, we'll have to forgive faster."

"You really are crazy."

"Why is forgiveness crazy?"

"Thinking I wanted Walter dead is crazy. I won't even talk to you on that level."

"Whoa," he says, and casts his line into the ocean. "We'll be out awhile."

· ★ ·

The sun is an amber ball floating above the fog bank on the horizon. The ocean turns dark, the line between ocean and sky more distinct.

A chill sets in, in the air, in Michael's limbs.

Against their boat flaps a stringer of fish, three ling cod, two red snapper, and a sea bass.

The look of concern on Andrew's face deepens.

"We have to go back when it gets dark."

"Who says?"

"It wouldn't be safe to stay out at night."

"Why not?"

"Well . . ."

"Repeat after me, Andrew. I wanted Walter to die so I could come home and marry his girl. It worked perfectly, except that it didn't. Because I felt like shit about it, and I've spent the last forty miserable years walking in his shadow."

"He was my best friend. I didn't want him to die."

"When I got hit with that mortar round, that was so close. Are you trying to say you never felt just the least bit disappointed that I pulled through?"

Andrew reels his line in, methodically, as if nothing can touch him or hurt him as long as he stays with a careful routine.

He never answers the question.

"Did you ever fantasize about me dying and you going home? Just run it through in your mind? How Mary Ann would be heartbroken, and you'd be there to comfort her, and you'd be the closest thing to me in her mind?"

"Everybody fantasizes."

233

Ah, he thinks. We're getting closer. "So part of you wanted me dead."

"I didn't kill you."

"But part of you wanted me dead."

"Maybe a very small part."

"Okay, Andrew. Here's the sixty-four-dollar question. Why didn't you push me out of the way?" The light has dwindled, he can't quite make out the expression on Andrew's face. Only the sky is still barely light now; the first stars glow. The pitch and roll of the boat has grown to feel normal. "When did you see the guy had me in his sights?"

"The same time you did."

"Exactly the same time?"

"Maybe a split second sooner."

"Why didn't you push me?"

"There wasn't time!" He screams it out, half standing, rocking the boat in a sudden, violent motion that causes him to splay his arms for balance and carefully sit down again.

"Reflexes not fast enough?"

"No, they weren't."

"I can't help wondering, though. What if you hadn't been in love with my fiancée? What if some little part of you hadn't wanted me dead? Would they have been just a little bit sharper?"

"If I answer that, are we done? Can we go back?" He stares aimlessly toward the horizon, showing Michael his profile.

"We're not even close."

"Well, it doesn't matter. Because there is no answer. Nobody can ever know that."

"But you live with the question, though. Don't you, Andrew?"

Andrew doesn't say.

· ★ ·

The sky is black now. Only the moon lights the night, throwing a stream of silver across the water.

Now and then, Michael picks up the oars and rows toward shore, to adjust for the current that would carry them away. The pier lights serve as his compass.

Andrew breaks the silence.

"Okay, I admit it. I wanted you dead."

"My God."

"Well, you asked me to say it."

"You son of a bitch."

"You are going to kill me, aren't you?"

"Andrew, goddamn it. When are you going to get this through your head? The whole problem is that I loved you like a brother. I could never hurt you. And you wanted me dead."

He finds himself half standing, shouting. Where is all that detachment now?

Then, like a spoken answer, he realizes that Walter is back running the show.

He feels oddly relieved.

Welcome back, buddy, he thinks to himself. I've gotten used to having you around.

Hope you're a forgiving sort.

CHAPTER THIRTY-FIVE

Walter

When I first meet Andrew, we're fourteen.

The Marx Brothers are in their heyday, talkies are obviously here to stay, and Nicky is no more than a clumsy ball of warm puppy fur, tripping over his own paws.

One night we slip out of our respective houses and meet down by the boardwalk late in the evening. Later than a fourteen-year-old would normally be out.

There's something about an ocean at night. Something wild. It's an untamable force, nothing at all like the beach on a summer day.

We lean on the rail and Nicky sits on my shoe, chews on one of the laces, and I let him.

I look up at the stars.

I don't know if it's baby stuff, wishing on stars, and I don't know Andrew too well, so why take chances?

Instead we just talk about the speed of light, and how we could be looking at stars that burned up a million years ago, and if so, which ones would that likely be?

I don't tell him it has anything to do with a star wish.

I just say, "If you could be anything when you grow up, what would you be?"

Know what he says?

"A soldier. Like my dad."

I say, "Why would you want to be anything like your dad?"

Because, you see, I know his dad, and he hits Andrew and screams at him and hits his mother, though I don't remind him of all these details just now.

"Okay, then I'll be a soldier like *your* dad."

Me, I can't answer. I really don't know.

So I pick out a star, without giving away that I'm doing it, and I say in my head, Star light, star bright . . . You know the rest.

I say, Please make Andrew a soldier, and please make me the kind of person who knows what I want to be when I grow up.

I want that night to do over. I can't have it. I can't have anything over again, that's just the problem.

We can drift around out here all night, but we can never change the way it all went down.

If I had it to do over again, just for the sake of conversation, I'd ask that Andrew please never be a soldier.

And I wouldn't waste my time worrying about what to be when I grow up.

I'd just wish to grow up.

CHAPTER THIRTY-SIX

Andrew

Andrew dangles one hand into the icy water.

He tries to think of the rolling of the boat, the light slapping of water on its sides, as a disturbance, not a lullaby.

He tries to stay awake. He lights a cigarette. It's his next to last one.

When he sees Steeb slip away, head nodding, he kicks Steeb's shoe, hard.

"If we fall asleep, we'll drift out to sea."

"Oh. Right."

Steeb sits up straight, rubs his eyes. Yawns.

It occurs to Andrew that it might have been a tactical error.

He should have let Steeb fall asleep, then slowly, methodically, pacing himself with care, tried to row for the pier.

Too late now.

"Okay," Steeb says. "Let's stay up. I'll tell you a story. Once upon a time there was a boy named Walter and a girl named Mary Ann."

"No. Not that one. Tell me the one about Walter's Purple Heart."

"You didn't want to hear that one from me."

"Just tell it."

"Why didn't you ask me in the hospital if you wanted to know?"

Andrew feels his temper slip away under stress. "Maybe I didn't want to know," he shouts, "but I do now, and I've been waiting forty years to hear this story, so give me something back for all this."

"Okay." Steeb takes up the oars, sights the pier lights, and straightens the boat, rowing to adjust for the drift. "Okay. We're in that cave, right? And somebody slams into me, and it turns me around. I'm not with you guys anymore. And then I hear Jay take it. Only I don't know yet it's Jay. I think it's you. I just couldn't go on through that."

"It was that much worse? Me over Jay?"

"Hell, yes it was. Andrew, I'd known Jay for a few weeks. I mean, I took his death hard and all, but—"

"No you didn't. You took it real well. Bobby, too. All you said about Bobby was that at least he got some first."

Steeb sets the oars, slips down until he sits on the floor of the boat, leans back on the bench. He runs his fingers through his hair and drops his head back, turning his face up to the sky.

"I handled it like I thought you'd want me to."

"How do you know what I wanted? It broke my heart to lose Bobby and Jay. Don't you think I would have liked a little commiseration?"

Steeb studies Andrew as if he can detect intricacies in the dark. In this light, Steeb looks older. Much older.

"So, maybe I underestimated you, Andrew."

"Go on with the story. You were upset that Jay died, even though he didn't die a virgin."

"No, no, you're mixing things up. I thought it was you. And Jay wasn't a virgin."

"I know, that's my point."

"No, I mean the night we all shared that—experience. Jay wasn't a virgin and neither was I."

"Wait a minute . . ." Andrew sits forward, as though folding his bulk over the knot in his belly will keep it in control. "We all were."

"No, Jay wasn't and I wasn't."

"How do you know about Jay?"

"He told me."

"Since when were you so tight with Jay that he told you things he didn't tell me?"

"Hey, don't get mad at me, Andrew. I didn't ask him to confide in me. He just did."

Andrew feels a wave of light-headedness. A result of hunger, he reasons. At least, that's the only reason he can bring himself to focus on.

"You said you were a virgin."

"I did not, Andrew, you did. You said it and you believed it."

"You told me you were a virgin when we met."

"Well, of course, Andrew, I was fourteen years old."

"And you never told me otherwise."

In the intervening silence, the slapping of the ocean seems amplified somehow. God, how he'd like to find dry land now.

"I couldn't tell you anything about me and Mary Ann. It was a very bad subject."

Andrew presses his eyes tightly shut, determined to talk through this, to function through it. He will not think about this. He will not feel it. He is not about to let this be true. His own sense of history will not be rewritten to accommodate it.

"She was your girlfriend. It was none of my business."

"You made it your business when you fell in love with her. You acted like it was your business from that point on."

"I'm surprised she didn't tell me about that before we got married."

"She assumed I'd told you, since we told each other everything. But we didn't, did we, Andrew? We withheld a lot. Didn't we?"

Andrew wipes his eyes, knowing the darkness will protect him. He wants this conversation to move on.

"Go on. You thought I was dead."

"So I panicked and ran. I was running away when I got hit. Running from you dying. I thought. From Bobby having died already. From shooting those two Japanese soldiers in the back. Not that you would ever understand that."

Andrew sighs, listens to the air pull into him, hears it leak out again, as though his life has broken down to fractions of seconds at a time.

"The first time I ever killed a man," Andrew says, "it was

in hand-to-hand combat. It was out in the light. On Papua, actually, after you were gone. At least, that's the first that I know for sure I killed. That I saw. I watched his eyes while he was dying. Then I almost turned the gun on myself."

"I'm sorry, Andrew, I didn't know."

"That was the problem with you, Crowley. You always thought you cornered the market on caring about things."

Steeb drops his head back and looks toward the stars again. A few minutes pass, and Andrew fears he's fallen asleep.

Then Steeb breaks the silence. "If I forgive you for wanting me dead, will you forgive me for running?"

"There's nothing to forgive. We were all scared."

"And for what happened with Mary Ann?"

"I'm the one that needs to be forgiven."

"Yeah," he says, "except for one thing. I'm still here. I'm blaming you for my death, but I'm here to tell you about it. I just can't get over the fact that I wanted to be Walter some more. I'm like a kid who can't adjust to change."

"Nobody can adjust to change. You never outgrow that."

"But life goes on. That's the funny part of all this. Even after I'm dead, life goes on."

"Forgiving isn't something you do overnight, Steeb. We'll starve to death before you get used to it."

"I guess you're right."

"Can we go back now? I'm hungry and I'm almost out of cigarettes."

Steeb picks up the oars and rows them in.

CHAPTER THIRTY-SEVEN

Michael

He drives in silence, Andrew at his right elbow, and on his left the sun comes up.

He feels a vague sense of disappointment. It's a vast sense, actually, but he's tired and burned out, and it feels vague. Somehow he thought the sun would come up on a new day. A new era.

It would be over. It wouldn't hurt anymore.

He turns in at the airport.

Andrew says, "Do you think we're done?"

"I don't know."

He thinks maybe it's another one of those things, like his

arrival at Andrew's door. It doesn't really solve anything, just sets the solution into motion. Hopefully.

He walks Andrew all the way to his flight gate.

He holds out his right hand, and Andrew shakes it.

"Thanks for believing me."

"I don't believe you."

Michael can't tell if it's a joke. Maybe not. Maybe it's possible to climb out of the foxhole and reclaim your atheism.

"You sounded like you did. Last night."

"If you knew anything," Andrew said, "if you had been there, you'd know Mrs. MacGurdy's cat was named Henrietta."

He laughs, and Andrew laughs, but it seems a function of fatigue. He still worries that Andrew is half serious.

"You're impossible."

"So I'm told, Steeb."

"Call your wife before you board. Tell her you're okay."

Just at that moment, his boarding call is announced.

"Maybe you could call her. Tell her what time I'll get in— 12:10. Got a pen? I'll give you the number."

"I know the number."

Andrew studies his eyes in a way that makes him squirm.

"I have to go."

"Right. Bye."

Damn, he thinks as he watches him walk away. Nothing has changed.

We still have nothing to say to each other.

· ★ ·

It's an hour later in Albuquerque, still she sounds rousted out of sleep.

"I'm sorry. Did I wake you?"

Her voice sounds gravelly. Hurt.

"I'm usually up by now. I had trouble sleeping. So. You survived your boat ride. Did Andrew come back, or are you the sole survivor?"

"No, he's fine. He's on his way home. He wants you to meet him at the airport—12:10." He turns his face to the window, watches Andrew's plane taxi toward the runway. "He's such a stubborn old man."

"Tell me."

"Wait. How did you know we were out on a boat?"

"Walter told me."

"Oh."

It sounds like an acceptable, everyday sort of occurrence, and he doesn't question it. But then, he's tired.

He closes his eyes briefly, feels the rhythmic pitch of the boat again. His body has memorized it.

She says, "So, what happened?"

"I don't know. Not quite what I expected. We went over all this stuff that seemed like a powder keg in my mind, but once we spit it out, it wasn't such a big deal."

"Maybe that was the point."

"Maybe. I thought everything would change. I thought I'd feel clear again, maybe get things back in perspective, and then when he left to come home to you, it wouldn't tear me in half." He feels tears start, can't stop them, doesn't try. There's something comforting about the strong, regular flow of tears, about allowing them to proceed unchecked. Through the blur, he sees Andrew's plane build up speed on the runway. "So he comes home to you, and then you just go on like nothing happened."

"No, not like nothing happened. Poor Michael. Poor darling. If you had told me a month ago that I could break a twenty-one-year-old's heart . . ."

"Yeah, well, now we're even."

The operator interrupts, asks for another seventy-five cents.

He's out of change.

"I have to go," he says, and hurries off the phone. Not because of the change—he could push that another minute. Because he doesn't want to know what comes next.

I'll call you? Make it easy on both of us and don't even write?

He doesn't want to discuss how much of an ending this is.

· ★ ·

Late that night, Michael has a dream. It's not one of the old-style dreams. Except in one very real sense it is. There is no war, no violence, no urgency. And yet, like the old dreams, it has far too many dimensions to resemble other dreams. To allow him to dismiss it as just a dream and nothing more.

In the dream, Michael sits in a very white kitchen with Walter and Millie. Both the mood and the kitchen are light and calm. Walter is dressed in his army uniform, but it's clean. Well pressed. New looking. Not rumpled or torn. His hair is neatly combed, his dark beard close shaven. Millie is about forty years old, sitting straight and tall. Her face looks impassive. She seems not really connected to the scene.

He looks at her, and she smiles at him. He looks at Walter, and Walter nods.

· ★ ·

When Michael wakes in the morning, he drives in to town to call Mary Ann from a pay phone. It might be too early, but this is important. Andrew might answer, but he has to do this all the same.

He closes his eyes, holds his breath as the phone rings.

Mary Ann answers. He breathes again.

"I'm sorry," he says. "Did I wake you?" He doesn't bother to tell her who it is. You never tell your lover or your best friend who it is. It's just you, and you just start talking.

"Not at all. I've been up for an hour. I was just about to send you a telegram."

"Mary Ann, I think Millie passed away."

A moment's silence on the line. Then she says, "That's what the telegram was going to say."

"I'm sorry. I know I need to get a phone."

"Well, I don't know. How often does something like this happen?"

"When's the funeral?"

"Day after tomorrow."

"Okay. I'll get there somehow."

"Michael, are you sure? You saw her before she died. Isn't that the important thing?"

"I'll find a way. I'll borrow money from Dennis. I'll fly standby." He sticks with the how to avoid addressing the why. Walter wants him to. It might be hard to explain.

"Michael. Just so you know . . . Andrew and I will be there. Together. Wouldn't that be unnecessarily hard on you?"

Michael breathes deeply. "Yes," he says. "Yes, it will be. See you day after tomorrow."

CHAPTER THIRTY-EIGHT

Walter

Okay.

For forty-three years, nobody but me and Andrew have known about this thing with Mrs. MacGurdy. But that doesn't matter anymore. We had a reason for keeping it a secret, but that reason is gone, over, out of date. So I'm spilling it right now.

Not that it was so dreadfully important in the great scheme of things, but I know you must be wondering, because Andrew and I were not the kind of guys who torture old ladies.

Anyway, here's how it all starts.

Here's where I am.

We're walking on the boardwalk on a Saturday night. There are five of us. Me and Mary Ann. A couple we know from school, even though we're all out of school now. The guy's name is Gary and the girl is Jeanette. It was Gary's idea to go out on a double date. Then Andrew got invited because Gary knew a girl for him. Then the girl chickened out. So poor Andrew is our fifth wheel.

I think he's a little uncomfortable about it, and that's why he had those three beers. The rest of us had maybe two, but we feel pretty okay. Andrew had three, and he doesn't hold that stuff so great anyway. He's a little plowed.

We're rolling along the boardwalk, just enjoying the night.

Andrew is making a point about baseball. About batters to be exact, and the difference between the good and the great. In his slightly plowed state, he gets pretty vehement about it. So he's walking backwards so he can get right in our faces with what he's trying to say.

And then he slams right into Mrs. MacGurdy. Almost knocks her down.

Now, if you were going to make yourself a list of all the neighbors you might dare to slam into, that list would begin with Andrew's mother and end with Mrs. MacGurdy. She is absolutely the most foul-tempered old lady anybody knows. She has some kind of spite thing going with the world, and all you have to do is cross her path wrong, and suddenly you're the world, and she'll let it off all over you.

Well, she lights into Andrew. Just humiliates him in front of everybody.

She says, "Oh. Andrew Whittaker. That makes sense. Learning to be a drunk like your father, I see."

Everybody stops. Stops walking, stops talking, stops smiling. The world just stops.

Andrew says, "I'm sorry, what did you just say to me?" He's been taught to be polite to his elders, but this is wearing the lesson thin.

"You heard me. I said your father is a drunken sadist, and your mother is a doormat who puts up with him, whatever, and I'm not surprised to see you grow up to be a juvenile delinquent. It's just what I'd expect from a family like that."

All this right in front of his friends.

Now, I would like to tell you that we all rally around and stand up for Andrew. I would love to tell you that. I'd like to rewrite history, but all I can really do is tell you the truth. We stand there with our mouths open, and she walks away, giving us dirty looks over her left shoulder.

After she's gone, we start slapping Andrew on the back and saying things like, "Hey, don't let that old bat get to you. What does she know?"

But he's mortified. We all are. And the night just sort of disintegrates.

I walk Mary Ann home.

When I get back to my house, Andrew's sitting on my front stoop. I know he can't go home and get to sleep, so I sit with him awhile.

"I'm going to kill her," he says.

"I wouldn't advise it."

"Why not?"

"They'll put you in jail."

"So? Might be worth it. I mean it. I'm going to hurt that miserable old witch."

"No, you don't get it, Andrew. Then you're just proving her point by being a juvenile delinquent. If you want to get back at her, make her look wrong."

"Oh, you want me to get back at her by being a good boy?"

"Well," I say. "We could make her look completely insane. And then if anybody hears about what she said, well, consider the source, right? Who listens to a crazy lady?"

So at least in that respect I improve things. At least I get him thinking about ways to hurt her that involve no blood or broken bones, and that won't land him in jail.

This is how it begins.

This is how we do it.

Every Monday and Thursday afternoon, Mrs. MacGurdy carries Angel down the basement stairs and does her washing. It takes more than an hour. She has one of those basements with the outside stairs, so Andrew can stand right at her back door and make sure she doesn't come into the house unexpectedly. If she comes up, the plan is he'll face her down and say he came to talk about what she did to him Saturday night. And I'll hear the commotion and go out the front door.

But she doesn't come up.

And while she doesn't come up, I slip into her house and very quietly—bear in mind her washer is loud, but I still try to be quiet—take every item in her house that isn't nailed down, and turn it over.

Her toaster. All the lamps. The clocks. Her big console radio. The candlesticks. The bowl of flowers on her table, which pours water all over everything. Her teakettle on the stove. Everything that turns over.

Then Andrew and I go back to my house and watch out the window, and pray, because for this to work right, she'll have to at least tell the neighbors. The best thing of all will be if she calls the police.

Less than two hours later, there's a police car in front of her house.

Now, we live in a quiet little town, and a police car in front of someone's house draws attention. Neighbors gather on the sidewalk to talk about what's going on.

Me and Andrew, we gather.

"What happened," I ask. "Did Mrs. MacGurdy get robbed?"

Mr. Blake from down the street, he says, "No, she claims nothing was taken. She claims somebody came into her house and turned everything upside down."

Me and Andrew, we burst out laughing, and Andrew says, "Right. Last week she told me she saw flying saucers hovering over her birdbath."

Now everyone's interested, and they gather around and say, Do you think she's crazy? And then they say, You know, I did think that was kind of strange, I mean who would do a thing like that? Go into somebody's house and turn everything upside down? I thought that sounded sort of crazy.

By the time we're done gossiping, somebody we don't even know comes up with some other Mrs. MacGurdy story that makes her sound pretty weird, and that makes it official. It's decided that she turned everything in her house over herself, just to get the attention.

From that day forward her first name is crazy. Crazy Mrs. MacGurdy.

It's kind of amazing how well it worked. It's kind of scary how quick your neighbors are to decide what you are, and how slow they are to ever change their minds about you. It's an eerie lesson in neighborhoods.

We did not do this for revenge. We did it to save the last of Andrew's dignity. No one cares what Crazy Mrs. MacGurdy says about you, or what she thinks.

Of course, it was only a partial solution. It didn't keep his father from being a drunken sadist or his mother from being a doormat. Actually, let's be honest with ourselves. It was no solution at all. She was not the only person to make that observation about Andrew's parents. Truthfully, if someone heard about that little incident on the boardwalk, they'd likely think, Well, she may be crazy as an old bat, but she's got those Whittakers to a tee.

But it allowed Andrew to pretend it was a solution. It made us feel as though we'd done something to put the world back to right.

The one condition was that we never, never, breathe a word to anybody that it was us. Because word travels. And then not only is the old lady vindicated as not crazy, Andrew is officially a juvenile delinquent. So we took an oath to take this to our graves.

And I did.

It's only forty years after I went to my grave that I'm bringing it out into the light.

As to that other thing you're wondering about, I'm right. The cat's name was Angel.

CHAPTER THIRTY-NINE

Michael

He stands with his hands clasped behind him, gazing down at his mother. Walter's mother. No, his mother. He doesn't know if there's a distinction anymore, or if it even matters.

He is standing in a funeral home in Ocean City. There is no formal funeral service going on, but more of a viewing. A room with an open casket, where loved ones come and go, view the body, pay their respects. The high windows over Michael's head are secular stained glass, a way of adding reverence to the scene. The carpet is dark maroon, thick, and soft. This is the kind of funeral, he thinks, that costs the family too much money. The casket, for example. Thousands of dollars' worth of craftsmanship, about to go into the ground. He wishes that the people who loved Millie had spent that money on her while she was alive.

But the body, now that's strangely beautiful. Even old and frail, skin papery, fingers bent with arthritis, there is beauty in Millie's face.

That's the way to go out, he thinks. Her body is spent, gone. Used as long and as hard as a body can serve. That's the time to leave.

Part of him envies her that.

He feels something swell up inside him, but it's not sadness. It feels more like celebration. He can't explain it, but it's welcome, and he allows it without question.

Then he remembers the funeral of his own mother, Michael's mother from this life. Remembers standing over her casket. Sixteen years old. The feeling is so much tighter, more closed up. No celebration. Nothing to really feel. Where has his ability to feel been hiding all these years?

He shakes that away, because it's too confusing. Comes back to Millie.

He lets one hand brush across the top of his head.

"I got a haircut." He smiles down at her, knowing she's not there, but still wanting to pay tribute to this left-behind Millie. "Love you, Mom."

He leans over and plants a kiss on the center of her cool forehead.

When he straightens up again, he sees a man standing close

to his side. Close enough to have heard him call her "Mom." The man seems concerned. Michael thinks he must be a close relative. Then it hits him.

"Are you Robbie?" Michael asks.

The man looks even more confused. He's a stocky man with coarse, thinning dark hair. The face is thick and jowly and altogether different. But the eyes. Those fierce eyes gave him away.

Now Michael knows why he had to come.

"Robb Crowley," he says. "Nobody has called me Robbie for a very long time. I know you, right?"

Robbie has not mentioned the "Mom" issue, but there is no doubt that he heard, and the tension of that certainty hangs over the proceedings.

"Do you feel like you know me?"

"What's your name?"

"Michael Steeb."

"Doesn't sound familiar."

"But something about me is. Right?"

"Yeah, I just can't place it. I mean, from where?"

Okay, Walter, Michael says in his head. I found him, now what do I do with him? I'll know? Right. Thanks. Helpful as always.

"I think you'd better ask Mary Ann or Andrew."

"They're not here yet."

"I know."

"No, really," Robbie says. "I'm curious. I want to know where I know you from. Why won't you tell me yourself?"

"Hey. Isn't that Aunt Patty and Uncle Dan?"

It is, he knows it is. He saw them several minutes ago. He

pulled it out of his hat to change the subject, but of course it only digs him in deeper. It wasn't a well-thought-out move.

Robbie's fierce eyes narrow. "Are you family? No, of course not. I'd know if you were. I don't get this. Why won't you tell me who you are?"

"Robbie—Robb. I just think this is not the kind of information that should come to you from someone you think you don't know very well."

Michael looks up to see Mary Ann and Andrew enter the room. Arm in arm. His resentment drops into a deep place in his stomach and sets up camp, feeling heavy and hard and unwelcome. He catches Mary Ann's eye, but she looks away as if ashamed.

"There she is," Michael says. "Go ask her."

Robbie stands in front of him for several more beats, staring. Then he breaks away to greet Andrew and Mary Ann.

· ★ ·

Sooner or later Michael has to approach them. It makes his stomach churn, but he decides to get it over with.

He walks up to where they stand.

Andrew looks him up and down, critically. Michael knows he isn't dressed well enough. He doesn't own a suit. Dennis loaned him a dark sport coat, but it's too big. And he's wearing it over jeans because he has no choice. It's all he has.

"Andrew," he says. "Mary Ann."

"Steeb," Andrew says. It doesn't sound like a compliment.

Andrew is holding Mary Ann's forearm so tightly with his own that she has to pry it free. His grip must have hurt her, but he seems to view it as a betrayal when she pulls away. He seems ripe to feel betrayed.

For a minute the two men just stand, nearly toe to toe, neither willing to break the gaze.

Then Mary Ann says, "Hey, you two. This is not the time or place for this."

Michael looks away. Sees Robbie across the room, still staring at him. Still trying to figure it out.

"What did you tell him, Mary Ann?"

He sees a split second of panic flash across her eyes. Maybe she thought he meant Andrew. What did you tell Andrew? About us?

"Who?"

"Robbie. Did he ask about me?"

"Excuse me," Andrew says.

Michael thinks he's interrupting, but it's just the opposite. He's excusing himself. He crosses the room and sits on a fabric-covered bench with his back against the wall. He folds his arms across his chest and sits watching. He doesn't take his eyes off them.

"Yes," Mary Ann says. "He asked me who you were."

"What did you tell him?"

"I said you were his big brother reincarnated."

"You did? What did he say?"

"I'm kidding, Michael. I didn't tell him that. How could I tell him that? I told him to meet me at the coffee shop on the corner by our motel. Three o'clock. I said it was a long story."

"He has no idea how long. Should I be there?"

"I don't know, Michael. I've never done anything like this before. Do you want to be there?"

Michael glances over at Andrew, who returns a hard stare. A resentment has built since Michael last saw him. He shouldn't be surprised. He dropped some heavy information about Walter and Mary Ann, and now it's had plenty of time to settle in.

"Does he know about us, Mary Ann?"

"Andrew?"

"Andrew."

"What part of us?"

"The recent part."

"I haven't told him," she says. "But that doesn't necessarily mean that he doesn't know."

· ★ ·

As he leaves the funeral home, stepping out into the cool, bright afternoon, he hears Andrew's voice behind him.

"Steeb."

He turns to see Andrew standing a few paces away.

Andrew says, "Whatever happened between you and my wife in the past, it's in the past. I don't care if it was 1942 or last week. It's still the past. And she's still my wife. We're done with this thing now. Go back to California and leave us alone."

Andrew turns and disappears inside the funeral home again, leaving Michael standing out on the street alone.

Yes, it is, Mary Ann, he thinks to himself. It's unnecessarily hard on me.

CHAPTER FORTY

Mary Ann

Mary Ann sits in a booth at the coffee shop, drinking tea and looking out the window. She misses this place. She feels she hasn't been happy a day since they left. If not for Andrew, she'd move back to Ocean City in a heartbeat.

She looks up to see that Robb has arrived.

She moves to stand, to embrace him, but he tells her not to bother. He leans over and kisses her cheek, then seats himself on the opposite side of the table.

They smile at one another. A bit nervously, she thinks.

"How are you holding up, Robb?"

"Okay," he says. "It was expected. She was so miserable

the last few months. I guess when it finally happened I realized I'd accepted it a long time ago. It's hard. I'm not saying it's not hard. But I'm okay."

The inevitable silence falls.

Mary Ann glances at her watch. Michael said he would be here. And now she feels she doesn't want to do this alone. Then again, it's only a couple of minutes after the hour. Maybe he'll be along soon.

Robb says, "Okay, enough with the mystery. This is killing me. Who is that guy?" He leans in close, as if to whisper a secret. "Want to hear something weird? He leaned into the coffin and kissed her on the forehead and called her Mom. How strange is that?"

"Well," she says, "not the strangest part of all this."

She glances at her watch again. Maybe he couldn't bring himself to show up for this. Maybe she's going to have to go it alone after all.

"There you go with the mystery again," he says. "Come on. Just tell me."

"Robb, Michael is a young man who showed up in our lives not too long ago, because . . . Well, because he needed to know more about Walter."

She sees a slight reaction on his face at the mention of Walter's name. A trace of flinch.

"What does he need to know about Walter?"

"Well, you know, I put that badly. Because he doesn't exactly need to know about Walter. Actually, he knows more about Walter than all the rest of us put together. It's more that he wanted to find some of the people that Walter knew."

"How does he know so much about Walter?"

"Well, that's hard to say. I guess it depends on what you believe. What you're willing to believe. The one thing nobody could dispute is that he remembers everything about Walter's past that Walter could possibly remember if he were alive right now."

Robb's eyes cloud over, and Mary Ann knows that he is retreating into himself. Building a wall.

"What do you mean, 'remembers'?"

"I don't know how to say it any better than that, Robb. I don't know how to do this. There's no rule book for this. Nobody I know ever had to do it before. I just don't know how I'm supposed to explain."

"Why don't you tell me," he says, a bit strained, "what *you* think is going on."

"My personal opinion?"

"Yes."

"I think that Walter has . . . come back."

She lets that sit on the table a moment, purposely avoiding his eyes.

"You honestly believe that."

"There's just too much that nobody else could possibly know. Let me put it another way, Robb. The reason it's driving you crazy, wondering who he is . . . It's because you felt like you knew him. Am I right?"

"Well, yeah, but—He probably just reminded me of somebody."

"Like Walter? Maybe he reminded you of Walter?"

They both look up to see Michael standing over the table, looking slightly out of breath.

"Sorry I'm late," he says. "Mary Ann. Robbie."

Robb pushes past Michael and out of the restaurant without so much as a word.

Michael sits down across from her, and they exchange a complicated glance.

"I can see *that* went well."

"Give him time," she says.

· ★ ·

Mary Ann and Michael step out onto the street together, turn right toward her motel. She has no idea where his motel is, if he even has one, but he seems to be walking her back.

"Sorry you had to do that alone," he says.

"It might have been even worse with you there. I don't know."

They hear a shout on the street behind them.

"Hey! You."

They stop and turn around. Robb is twenty or thirty paces behind them, standing with his legs apart, the way he used to do as a kid when he was mad. That "you can't knock me down" pose.

Mary Ann realizes he has been following them, and it seems funny and sad and touching all at once, because it's such a throwback to older times. Walking through Ocean City with Walter only to find that the kid brother is tagging along a few paces behind, often with an agenda. She wonders if Robb sees the irony. She figures he probably doesn't.

He even looks childishly angry, though the rest of him is clearly middle aged.

"Tell me something only Walter would know," he says, coming a few steps closer.

Michael seems to roll that over in his brain for a moment. Then he smiles. He extends two fingers and brings them up to his eye level, touching his forehead briefly.

"How about the finish-line salute?"

Mary Ann has no idea what the finish-line salute is, but she gathers that Robb knows.

He turns and slips around the corner like a young boy running away.

CHAPTER FORTY-ONE

Walter

Here's the scene.

Andrew is standing on my front lawn. On crutches. Trying to get up the nerve to go to the door. Trying to face Millie in light of what just happened.

Well, not just. But this really brings it all home, doesn't it?

He already faced her on the phone but I'm guessing this feels different. He sure acts like it does. He acts frozen. Like somebody put him in a deep freeze, and now it would take him an hour to move a muscle. If he could move any muscle at all.

Now his eyes land on the star. The gold star my parents put in our front window, so the whole town will know they lost a son to the war. Like the whole town doesn't know already. But anyway, that's what people do.

Poor Andrew. I don't think he was ready for that. He drops the crutches and falls to one knee. The good one. He has one that's so bad it was his ticket home. Even though he didn't come down on it, I think just bending it must be a painful thing. He doesn't act like he noticed that.

I keep thinking he's going to cry, but he doesn't. It's like he's got the whole sorrow thing down, all except the tears. Now that I think about it, I never saw Andrew cry. I guess I never will.

My mom sees him out the window. She throws open the door, and Nicky comes running out, comes right to me. He's so happy to see me. And vice versa, believe me. Maybe "see" is the wrong word. Does he see me? I don't know. I don't know much about the inside of a dog. But he's spinning around in circles and jumping up. If I were really here, body and all, he'd be jumping on me, just like dogs have jumped on their people since the beginning of the world as we know it. Only he's jumping at nothing as far as anyone can see.

My mom comes out to where Andrew is kneeling on the lawn. She drapes herself over his back, and they cry together.

Except Andrew doesn't cry.

"Look, Andrew," she says through the tears. She points at Nicky. "Look how happy he is to see you."

Neither one of them seems to notice that Nicky hasn't looked at Andrew once.

· ★ ·

Now we're all in the kitchen, and Andrew is halfway through his second piece of pie. The one he's supposed to eat for me. It's kind of not fair, though, because he doesn't appreciate it properly. He's always thought lemon pie was "okay." No better than a cookie or some vanilla ice cream. Though maybe the piece he's eating for me tastes better.

My mom says, "Have you called Mary Ann?"

Andrew's face gets red, and he looks down at the table like he's just been caught doing something wrong.

"No, ma'am. Not yet. We've been writing, and I told her I was coming home. But I haven't called yet, no."

"Well, why not? You know she'll want to see you."

"Think so?"

My mom sighs and walks over to the phone, which is on the wall near the refrigerator. My dad got her a new phone while I was away, I guess. I think he's been giving her a lot of stuff. I see new stuff everywhere. A new stove. A new couch. Seems like he's bought her everything but what she lost.

She's talking to the operator, and Andrew looks like he's going to fall right through the floor.

"Is Mary Ann there? Thank you." She smiles at Andrew, who looks away again. "Mary Ann. You won't believe who I've got here. That's right. Right here in my kitchen, I swear. Why don't you come to dinner tonight? I'm making a couple of roast chickens. They're big chickens, there'll be plenty. Yes, I'll hold on to him. Great. See you at six."

· ★ ·

After dinner, Mary Ann offers to help my mom with the dishes. My mom won't hear of it. She's trying to keep those two together. But Mary Ann insists on at least clearing the table.

I'm with them in the kitchen when my mom says, "Mary Ann. Honey. Please don't take this the wrong way. But maybe it's time for the engagement ring to come off now. You're still a young woman."

Mary Ann just stands there with her mouth open. From the look on her face my mom might just as well have suggested we put Robbie out with the trash or use Nicky to get a good blaze going in the fireplace.

She opens her mouth like she's going to say something, but nothing comes out.

"Just think about it, dear," my mom says. "Just think about what I said. Sooner or later you'll have to."

Then she ushers us all back into the living room and says, all loud and cheery, "I didn't make any dessert, so Andrew, you'll have to take Mary Ann out for an ice cream."

Everybody knows there's three-quarters of a nice fresh pie in the kitchen. But Andrew is being a total dolt.

He says, "Oh, that's okay. I'm stuffed. Really."

My mom shoots him a look that says, Wake up. "But maybe Mary Ann would like an ice cream."

He meets her eyes and gets the message. "Oh. Right. I'll take her down to the boardwalk for one."

Everybody shakes their head a little. My dad. My mom. Me.

· ★ ·

Now the three of us are leaning on the railing, along with Andrew's crutches, looking out to sea in the dusk. Well, two of us are leaning. And two of us are full of ice cream. But we're all here.

Guess what the topic of conversation has been? All evening?

It started the minute we left the house.

Mary Ann said, "I want to hear every detail, every single minute of everything that happened in the war."

So Andrew opened his mouth and started spilling it all, but by the time we got down to the boardwalk it was clear that Mary Ann had neglected to add the phrase "as it relates to Walter," because, I guess, she felt it went without saying.

Now an hour has gone by in that mode, and we're at the rail, staring at the fishing boats in the dusk.

Mary Ann looks up to watch the seagulls circle. She says, "Remember how he used to feed them bread out of a brown paper sack? They always got all excited, like they are now. I wonder why they're all excited now."

Andrew shrugs. "I guess seagulls are excitable."

Mary Ann seems not to have heard. She says, "He was always so sure they knew him. Like, when they were all swooping around screaming like this, he said that was probably their way of saying, 'Look. Here comes the bread guy.' You don't suppose they know us, do you? From being down here with him so many times?"

"Um. I don't know," Andrew says. "Maybe." But you can tell he doesn't mean it. You can tell his whole current life is making him uneasy. Mary Ann doesn't seem to notice, though.

"Tell me about when he died."

That sits on the rail for a while, making Andrew doubly uncomfortable.

"You don't want to hear about that."

"Yes I do."

"Why?"

"Because it was him. It was part of his life. I know all about the rest of his life. Now I need to know that part. I know it was ugly, but you need to tell me about it anyway."

"It wasn't ugly."

"It must have been. How can that be pretty?"

"It was just a little bullet hole. He was just there one minute, and then he was on the ground with this tiny little bullet hole. It wasn't hard to look at. Not at all. He looked peaceful."

"A year ago I could never have brought myself to talk about this. But I'm handling things better now."

They're quiet for a long time, just looking out over the water.

Then Mary Ann turns to him and smiles. That smile that just lights up her whole face. Lights up the whole boardwalk, for that matter.

"This has been so nice," she says.

"Really?"

"Oh, I've just enjoyed myself so much with you tonight, Andrew."

"Really? I mean, thanks. Yeah. Me, too. This has been really nice."

She links her arm through his in a sort of brotherly-sisterly way.

"I mean, you were his best friend. You were with him every minute. Right up until the minute he died. I haven't had anybody I could talk about him with. It's been so long since I got to talk about him like this."

Andrew nods a little, and dredges up a smile that makes him look slightly seasick.

He says, "We should do this again sometime, then."

"I'd love to. Any time. There's still so much I want to ask. As soon as I get home I'll think of a million things I meant to ask you about him."

Now, I'm sure I'm destined to forget it many times over, but right at this moment, I see it very clearly. I see that there's no need to punish Andrew for coming home to my girl.

I see that his punishment is all in place, and it isn't going anywhere anytime soon, and nothing I could dream up to hurt him would even come close.

CHAPTER FORTY-TWO

Michael

Michael flies back standby, and it takes him two days to get home.

He can't afford a motel, so he lives at the Albuquerque airport for the requisite time, waiting for a flight that isn't overbooked. Then he lives at Los Angeles International for a little while longer.

When he finally gets in, there's no one he can call to come pick him up at the airport and drive him home. He didn't drive his van to the airport. He was so broke from the standby ticket that he couldn't afford the long-term parking.

So Dennis drove him. He had no real plan for the return trip, but it seemed less important at the time.

He has to hitchhike home. Rides don't come easily, so he walks a big part of the way with his bag.

He arrives on his own front porch ready to kiss the bare, unfinished planking.

"Yo, Dennis," he calls as he steps into the house. "Can you believe this? I actually made it home."

Dennis stands on the upstairs landing, looking down.

"You look tired," he says.

"Oh, my God, you have no idea. Tired hardly says it. I've been traveling forever. I haven't slept right for days. And I've barely eaten, because I ran out of money. I must've walked fifteen miles with this damn bag. I am so happy to be home I could just cry. I am never moving from this place again."

Dennis says, "Hey, while you were gone—"

"No, don't even hit me with that yet, okay? I'm going to take a hot shower for about a year. I'm going to sleep until I wake up and then do nothing but play sax until I get my energy back. I can't handle anything else right now."

Dennis comes down the stairs to where Michael is standing. He looks far too empathetic. He must know something Michael doesn't.

"Then I'm extra sorry to have to tell you this," he says. "But Mary Ann called and said Andrew's in the hospital."

"Wait. Called . . . where?"

"Well, she got smart and called the post office and talked to our mail guy. Asked him to give you a message to call. But you weren't here, of course. So I went into town and called her myself. Told her you must be having trouble getting back."

"Wait. Andrew is in the hospital . . . why?"

"I didn't ask."

"You didn't ask why?"

"No, should I have?"

"Well, it seems kind of basic, Dennis. Is he doing okay?"

"I didn't ask." Dennis defends himself against Michael's eyes rolling. "Hey, I barely even met the old guy. You're the one who's so close all of a sudden. I gave you the message. Quit bagging on me."

"Okay, Dennis," he says, sitting heavily on his duffle bag. "What exactly *did* you ask?"

"If she wanted you to come out there."

"Does she?"

"Desperately. She knows it's too much to ask, but she needs you like never before. She didn't say it in those exact words, but that's exactly what she meant. Take my word for it."

Michael purposely falls over backwards onto the wood floor, arms spread in an impromptu crucifixion.

"I'm going to die," he says.

"Go to Albuquerque first. I sold some product while you were gone. Some of the stuff we put aside. So you'd have gas money."

"We were saving that until the prices went back up. That was supposed to be for the electrician."

Dennis shrugs. "We'll live."

"*You'll* live," Michael says. "I'm going to die." But before Dennis goes back upstairs, Michael also says, "Thank you."

He lies there for a while, on his back on the floor.

He thinks he'll take that long, hot shower first. But he realizes that he has no clean clothes anyway. Not in his duffle bag, not in his drawers. And he doesn't have the time or the energy to drive into town to the laundromat. And it seems pointless to get clean just so he can put on dirty clothes.

He'll just have to shower and do laundry when he gets there.

He gets up off the floor, washes his face and armpits, eats an avocado sliced onto a piece of wheat bread.

Then he throws his bag into the van, takes the gas money from Dennis, and hits the road.

"Please make it," he says to the van as he pulls out of the driveway. "Please get all the way there. If you just do this one thing for me, I swear I'll never call you a piece of shit again."

· ★ ·

Every fifty miles or so he stops at a gas station, tops off his radiator, and calls Mary Ann. Every time he calls, he lets the phone ring twenty times, but she's not home. She's obviously at the hospital.

Which hospital, Dennis? he thinks. Oh, that's right. You didn't ask.

Every time he stops to call her, he buys a cup of coffee. But that will only serve him for just so long. Sooner or later he will have to stop over for the night and sleep.

At eleven o'clock that night he finally reaches Mary Ann at home.

"Oh my God, you're home," he says. "Are you okay?"

"Michael. Where are you?"

"Almost halfway there. Are you okay?"

"Oh, Michael. You're coming. You're a prince."

"I'm a very tired prince, Mary Ann. I have to sleep. I can't go another mile tonight. I have to sleep and start over in the morning."

"Of course you do. Sleep. Don't get into an accident."

"What happened?"

"He had a heart attack."

"But he's alive, right? How does it look?"

"Hard to tell at this point."

"I have to see him, Mary Ann. I can't be too late."

"Just sleep, Michael. You can't do more than you can do. I think you're just wonderful for trying. Just get a good night's sleep and do your best."

· ★ ·

After he hangs up the phone he buys another cup of coffee and gets back on the road.

CHAPTER FORTY-THREE

Walter

I can think of so many compelling reasons to be Walter. I just know I'm going to miss that when it's gone.

No doubt you've gathered by now that I'm a pretty ordinary guy. Other than being good at track and relatively easy on the eye, there's nothing so remarkable about me. Except that I'm Walter. And I'm Walter in a way that nobody else ever has been before or ever will be again. And I honestly believe that Walter-ness counts for something. No more than anybody else's them-ness counts, but that's exactly the point I'm trying to make.

Michael is all excited now about the fact that life goes on

and he's still here. It just recently struck him that nothing ends, and that there's a real sense of safety in reincarnation. Okay, it's true, nothing ends. But everything changes. And in those changes something is gained but something very important is lost.

Like me.

I shouldn't be feeling sorry for myself now that I'm finally about to move on. And I'm not, really. It's more that I'm noticing the value of what I was given now that I have to give it back.

I'd like to tell you that I properly appreciated every single moment of the life I was given, but I'm just like everybody else. Most of the time I forgot to bother.

But sometimes it broke through. I can look back now and see the whole ride, and those moments stand out like sunlight reflecting off the Atlantic Ocean. One little sparkle each.

That early morning trip in the back of my neighbor's pickup truck. Remember? I told you about that.

And the time I'm driving my dad's '39 Ford, shifting up through the gears, and I come into this curve that's just enough of a curve that I really have to lean a little with it. Well, not have to. The car doesn't care if you lean, but anyway, that's what you do. Something about my hands on the wheel and my feet on the pedals and my body shifting into the curve, it's like there's no separation between me and the car. No way to tell where Walter leaves off and Ford begins. We're working together like one machine. So I have eight cylinders of gasoline combustion, and it's so much power. So much power and speed. Makes me think I can have the world. Or at least my own little corner of it. It only lasts a second, but what a second.

And the time I'm swimming in the ocean, and I'm trying to get out beyond the waves. Maybe I'm nine. I don't know, but I'm definitely little. I feel little. And a wave washes over me and tumbles me over and over and holds me down. I'm struggling to get back up, but the natural world is so much stronger. So I know then that I can't fight. I'll die if I fight. So I just let go and work with the ocean, and sure enough it pops me back up into the air, and I breathe. Gasp in all this wonderful oxygen, with saltwater running off my hair and into my mouth.

Then I go back to shore and lie on the sand on my towel and feel the sun drying up the little beads of water one by one. I can see the sunlight even with my eyes closed, and I can hear voices on the boardwalk, and it all seems louder and brighter and more wonderful because just for this moment I know enough to be happy I'm here.

You think you'll never forget again, but then you do.

And there's even a Mary Ann moment in there. When we're parked in my dad's car, but still in the front seat. And we're kissing in a way that's still relatively polite, but then all of a sudden our mouths are open just a little bit and our tongues touch. It's a surprise, because it's so much of our individual aliveness coming together. It seems to multiply in that split second, and between the two of us, we're just so alive I can hardly stand it.

Just in that split second I forget to guard against losing her, or her losing me. Just for that instant I forget to hold this other perfect human being at arm's length because our chance is almost over.

Probably I should have told her that, but where would I have found the words?

Even now I'm not explaining it right. Any of this. It's so much bigger than the words. You have to squeeze it down small to fit it into the words, and then it's like a shadow of what you know you felt.

But it's my last chance to tell you these things, so I have to try.

Then there are even smaller, stupider things. Well, they're not stupid, really. I guess I just worry they'll sound that way.

Like waking up at night with Nicky's head on my neck. Feeling all that warm fur, and a little bit of his breath on my ear. And he twitches a little. Makes a little whimper noise in his sleep, so now I know that dogs dream, but I fall back asleep wondering what they dream about.

And a really hot day, when I pick up a bottle of Coke, and it's cold in my hand, and my hand goes around it just right, like they made that bottle specially to fit there. And the first slug goes down, and it tastes just like I want it to, and I can feel the cold move down through me. It makes me remember I have a body in a way I don't think I otherwise would.

And running so hard and so fast that it feels as if my heart is going to burst, but it doesn't. It opens up a little bit more.

And of course that first bite of warm lemon pie.

These are the moments when I looked through to the other side and really knew what I had in being alive. But now, looking back, every moment feels equally important. Now the most tedious and uneventful day I ever spent feels like a gift.

Now I'm holding those moments like a heaping double handful of pearls, and at the same time I'm admiring their beauty, I have to open my hands and let them pour through.

CHAPTER FORTY-FOUR

Michael

Andrew's eyes are open when Michael comes into his hospital room. Blank, weak, but open.

"Hey, buddy," Andrew says. "I knew you'd be here."

His voice is a scratchy whisper in his throat, as if he hasn't the breath to really push it out.

Michael moves quietly toward Andrew's bed, slowly, as if afraid of waking him from this dream.

"You called me buddy."

"So? Big deal. I always call you that."

"Andrew, do you know who I am?"

"Of course I know who you are, you big jerk."

Michael takes Andrew's hand, looks hard into his eyes, holding back tears at the vacancy he sees.

Andrew's skin seems pasty, his eyes too deeply set, as if re-treating.

Andrew says, "Lots of guys are afraid of dying, but not me. I said to myself, I said, Andrew, you got a buddy on the other side. He'll be there for you. And here you are."

"Don't talk, buddy," Michael says. "Save your strength."

"What for? It doesn't matter now, right? At first I thought to myself, Maybe my old buddy doesn't forgive me. But I know now. All that stuff is gone. It doesn't cross over with you. Am I right?"

Michael pats his hand, wanting to quiet him.

"I think you are, buddy. There's only one problem with that. You're not dead."

"I'm not? Oh, shit."

Andrew goes quiet now, in a defeated sort of way, closes his eyes.

Michael sits with him until Mary Ann comes.

· ★ ·

"What happened, Mary Ann? God, this is all my fault."

He looks up from his chair to see her standing over him, an exhausted angel, dark circles under her eyes from lack of sleep.

Andrew is sleeping deeply, but Michael pulls Mary Ann out into the hall just to be safe.

She says, "Of course it isn't your fault, Michael, don't be silly."

She reaches for him, and he allows himself to be held, reluctantly at first, still jittery with worry, then desperately, like a man about to break. Like a man who needs outside help to hold himself together.

"He had a heart attack, Michael. It's not his first. It's not your fault."

"Oh, I said some awful things, Mary Ann. When we were out on that boat. I really shook him up with some of the things I said."

"You couldn't have said anything he'd never thought of on his own."

He pulls back away from her, hesitantly, drawing back into his own skin.

"When Dennis said he was in the hospital, I thought he tried to commit suicide."

Mary Ann shrugs. "Well? What would you call it? He smokes two packs a day of filterless, drinks too much, won't eat anything that isn't deep fried. And this is after two other heart attacks. He's been going like that since the war. Ever hear the one about the man who commits suicide by tying his neck to the rafter and standing on a block of ice?"

He turns his eyes to hers, a little wounded. She sounds callous, unsympathetic, though he knows it's probably not how she feels. It's probably the shield she's been using to get by.

"Is he going to be okay?"

"It looks good at this point. No guarantees."

"If you could have heard some of the things I said to him on that boat, Mary Ann. God, if I had that to do over . . ."

"What could you have said that was so terrible?"

"I got him to admit that he wanted Walter to die."

She seems to take a moment to right herself. As if she's been hit. Almost knocked off balance.

"He admitted to that?"

"Eventually, yes."

"Why would he want Walter to die?"

"Because he loved you. He wanted to come home and marry you."

"Oh. We better go back inside."

· ★ ·

Andrew's eyes are wide open as they approach his bedside. He turns his face to Michael.

"Steeb." Andrew's face fills with exaggerated contempt. "What are you doing here?"

"Honey," Mary Ann says, crossing quickly to his bed, "Michael came all the way from California to see you. Isn't that nice?"

"Yeah, swell."

Michael smiles. "Glad to see you back to yourself, buddy."

"I'm not your buddy, Steeb."

CHAPTER FORTY-FIVE

Mary Ann

They sit quietly in back of her well-tended home, Michael surveying her backyard in the moonlight. She sees it through his eyes now, the neatly clipped grass, the border of garden. The carefully trained roses climbing the wooden fence. Ferns and flowering plants, ivy on trellises.

"Your garden is beautiful," he says.

"Thank you."

She is sipping at a glass of red wine, and as she comes close to finishing it, Michael reaches over and fills her glass again.

It's late, after dark, and the air has finally become cool.

Barely cool. It feels like breathing for the first time in years.

"I can tell you put a lot of time into it," he says. "That you love it. You can always tell what someone loves, because they pay attention to it. No matter what you say you love, what you really love is what you put the most time into." He pauses for a big breath, seeming shy, as if he feels he's talking too much. Then he plunges on anyway. "Sometimes I look at my life and think, What do I really care about? What's important to me? I think when I get home I'm going to finish building that damn house."

She says nothing, just takes hold of his hand.

He pulls her out of her chair and onto his lap. She doesn't argue or resist. He wraps his arms around her waist, and she lays her head on his shoulder.

"I'm not trying to start with you," he whispers in her ear.

"I know."

He buries his face in her hair, against her neck. "I don't want him to die, Mary Ann."

"Are you sure?"

He pulls her head off his shoulder to look at her face. His face is in shadow. It doesn't tell her what she wants to know.

"I'm positive. I just found him again, after all this time. I don't want to lose him."

"But you wanted us to be together so much."

"Not like that. Not at the expense of his life."

She scrutinizes his face at close range, to satisfy herself of his sincerity. Then she says, "You see, that's what Andrew should have said."

"What do you mean?"

"About Walter. That's how he should have felt. I've been thinking about it all day. Ever since you told me. Trying to convince myself it was just human. That any human being would feel that way. But I can't believe it. All those months I spent at home, praying Walter would come back safe. And Andrew was hoping he wouldn't. It feels like a betrayal. Like something the enemy would do."

He sighs, lays her head back against his shoulder. Strokes her hair.

"You have to forgive him for that, though."

"Why?"

"Because that's what it's all about, I think. I think that's what he needs us to do."

"What about what I need?"

"Walter, I mean. What Walter needs us to do."

"Oh."

"I think that's why we're doing this. Running this all over again. So we can forgive each other. I think."

"I don't know, Michael." She sniffles lightly. "Maybe not that. I don't know if I can forgive that."

They sit quiet for a long time. Several minutes.

Then Michael says, "You and Andrew never had kids, huh?"

"No."

"He didn't want them?"

"No, he did."

"Why, then?"

"I didn't want them."

"You're kidding. You said you wanted five or six."

"I think I said four or five," she says, sipping at her wine again. "I meant Walter's kids. I meant I wanted to have four or five kids with Walter."

"Wow," Michael says. "That had to hurt him."

"I never told him straight out why not. Some part of him might have known, though. And there was another reason. Andrew would have been a lousy father. He didn't see that, but I did. He was so critical. Growing up with Andrew would have been a lot like growing up with Andrew's father. He'd kill me if he heard me say that, but it's true. He thinks he's so different from his father."

"Yeah," Michael says. "We all like to think we're different from our parents. I have to go talk to him tomorrow," he says. "If he's awake. If he's okay. God, I hope he'll be okay. I hope I'm not too late."

He probably wants to hear her say she hopes so, too, but he doesn't push. She's angry at Andrew, and she guesses Michael can feel it. Maybe the kind of angry that doesn't go away. Maybe she wishes he'd never told her. No, it was right. All of this was right.

She needs to be angry with Andrew anyway, if only for tying his neck to the rafter and standing on a block of ice.

He holds her until the night becomes cold and unwelcoming, until a light chill sets in along her feet and arms.

Then she makes him a bed on the couch, and he accepts it without question.

· ★ ·

An hour later, he sticks his head through her open bedroom doorway. Sees her looking back at him.

"I can't sleep," he says. He sounds like a little boy trying to climb into bed with his parents. "Can I just come in and talk?"

"Of course."

He lies down on the bed beside her, on top of the covers and respectfully apart.

He says, "Something keeps bothering me. I can't stop thinking about it. Remember right before we left the hospital tonight? He kept saying he wanted to go home."

"He was on a lot of drugs."

"I know. But I wonder. Something about the way he said it. And you kept saying, 'Well, pretty soon, dear, if you'll just concentrate on healing,' and he kept saying, 'No, no, you don't get it. I want to go home.'"

"He's just not very lucid right now, is all."

She rolls toward him. She wants to be close to him, wants to use him for comfort.

Most of all, she wants him not to say what he's about to say.

"Maybe he wasn't talking about home, as in here."

"You mean Ocean City?" She knows he doesn't.

"No, I don't think so."

The phone rings. They both jump, both sense the immediate threat.

She glances over her shoulder at the clock. It's after midnight.

"Anybody ever call you this late?"

"No, never."

It rings again, then again.

They stare at it, as if it will back down at their obvious willingness to defend.

But it doesn't stop ringing.

CHAPTER FORTY-SIX

Andrew

He feels the presence of someone over his bed. A nurse, most likely.

It's late. Dark. Shift change, maybe.

He opens his eyes.

He's still not sure what he sees. He'll need time to adjust to the light.

A young man, that much he can tell. Not a nurse. "Steeb?"

"Guess again, buddy."

He knows the voice. The features come clearer now, as his eyes adjust. The heavy stubble, the cleft chin. Those eyes.

"I knew you'd be here," Andrew says. He feels relieved.

It's over. He can rest now.

"Here? Here where, buddy?"

"You know. Here."

"Andrew. We're in Albuquerque."

"Oh. Oh, no." He feels something unfamiliar, something hot and irritating behind his eyes. Tears. How long have they been away? Since he was twelve? Younger? Ten, maybe. Since the last time his father called him a baby and slapped his mouth for crying, but he can't remember when that was. "What do I have to do, Walter? I want to go home. What do I have to do to go home?"

Walter perches on the edge of his bed. There's an eagerness now, in his tone.

"I'm glad you asked me that question, Andrew. Are you sure you're ready?"

"I was ready years ago."

"You have to open up your mind."

"To what?"

"Well, for starters, everything you heard from Steeb."

Andrew drops his head back to the pillow, sighs.

"I believe him. I have to. What choice have I got? There's no other explanation. I knew when I first got a good look at his eyes."

"Which was . . . ?"

"You know, when I was at his house that night."

"Why didn't you look at his eyes when he first came to your door? She did. She knew."

Andrew pulls in a sniffly breath, wipes his cheeks with the backs of his hands. The tears are coming faster now. They're out of control. Everything is. Suddenly his life is a speeding car with no steering. Is that good or bad? He almost likes it.

"I didn't want to believe in reincarnation."

"And you still don't, right, buddy? Or this would be over. Why not? What hurts about believing?"

He thinks he won't answer. That he doesn't know. That he wouldn't open up if he did know, because he never has. But the answer happens, almost without him.

"I don't want to do it all over again." Walter scratches his chin, nods slightly. "It's the cruelest joke of all, Walter. When it's finally over we have to do it again. I'm tired. I just want to rest. Isn't there someplace I can go to rest?"

"Sure, buddy. You can come over to this side. If you want to rest, you can take a century. An eon. The time you can take if you need it, you can't even imagine it. You don't even know that much time exists."

"But you came back right away. Not even twenty years to get born again."

"My choice, buddy. I turned around as fast as I could. I wanted to catch you on your way out. I mean just on your way out. I knew you wouldn't believe it until right about now. When you're so close you can almost see me. That is how you break an old fool. I'm stuck, Andrew. I need you. I need your help. It's like I can't let go of what happened, so I'm stuck."

"What do mean, 'stuck'? Stuck on what?"

"Grudges, buddy. They're like anchors. If you're holding one, you're going nowhere."

"Are you sure you can unstick now?"

"Couldn't be more positive. With your help, I am now officially out of here."

"So what do I have to do to come with you?"

"You already did it, buddy. Everything that needs doing. Thanks for sending my stuff to Michael. That was a nice touch. You can rest now."

Andrew rolls over to face the wall. He feels sleepy. He wants to curl up into a catnap, never hear an alarm, never feel a hand shake his shoulder.

He feels a seizing in his chest, a familiar searing pain. He tries to breathe around it, but it's too big. It radiates along his left arm, folds him in half, like he's a piece of trash too big for disposal.

He tries to cry out, to call somebody. Not to save him, just to ask them to take the pain away. Make it not hurt.

Not just his chest.

Everything.

He hears Walter's voice close to his ear. "Don't worry, Andrew, it only hurts for a minute."

And he's right.

Now it doesn't hurt anymore.

Not just his chest.

Everything.

CHAPTER FORTY-SEVEN

Walter

I have to go now.
Bye.

CHAPTER FORTY-EIGHT

Michael

Michael readies himself slowly, numbly, willing his hands to work with every motion.

He dresses in a suit borrowed from Andrew's closet.

It's too long in the sleeves, so he practices in front of the mirror, keeping his elbows bent, folding his arms across his chest, to keep the sleeves up above his knuckles.

He combs his hair in the mirror, examines his own face, the way he'd watch a stranger. He has circles under his eyes. He looks old. Tired.

He finds Mary Ann in her bedroom, fussing with her hair as if it mattered.

He pushes up against her from behind, slides his arms around her waist. He watches her face in the mirror. She doesn't. She leans back on his shoulder, squeezes her eyes shut.

"Thank God you're here, Michael. I don't know how I'd do this if you weren't here."

"You're going to be okay. We both are."

"I know," she says. "But right at this moment I'm not."

"You want me to drive?"

"No, it's okay. Robb's coming to pick us up."

"You're kidding."

"No, he insisted."

"I didn't even know he was that close with Andrew. To come all the way in from Dallas for the funeral."

"I think Andrew might be only part of it. I think he wants to see you."

· ★ ·

Michael sits in the backseat of Robbie's rented car, looking at the back of Mary Ann's head.

She reaches a hand over the back of the seat and Michael holds it. Then he takes off his seat belt so he can lean forward and kiss the back of her hair.

Robbie is watching them from the corner of his eye.

Michael sits back. Catches his eyes in the rearview mirror.

"So, Robbie," he says. "You didn't take the store."

"Excuse me?"

"Crowley and Sons Hardware. You didn't take it. Mary Ann tells me you're an investment broker."

"I was a hardware man until the day Dad died," Robbie says. "I advertised the store for sale the next day."

Michael notices that he said "Dad." Not "My dad." Just "Dad." He figures that might be some kind of progress, and that he had best not push for any more right now.

· ★ ·

He walks Mary Ann through the front door of the church, one hand on her arm, one behind her back, like a brace. Most of the family and friends have already arrived.

They're late, not that it matters.

Hands reach out to her as they pass, squeeze her arm or her free hand.

Michael tries not to monitor the faces around him. He doesn't know who most of these people are. They don't know who he is; he can tell. But he can live with not knowing, and they seem curious.

The casket is open. No lies, no secrets.

Andrew looks unreal somehow, too good, which makes him look terrible.

Michael watches Mary Ann, but she doesn't cry. She will. When she's ready, she will.

She kisses Andrew's former outer self lightly on the forehead.

When she seems done, when it doesn't seem like interrupting, Michael does the same.

"So long, buddy," he whispers, one thin notch above silence.

He wonders, if Andrew could hear him, would he argue with that assessment? Or would he concede that Michael is his buddy?

· ★ ·

The sun beats down on the cemetery, and Michael loosens his tie slightly. It's ninety-five degrees in the sun, and the black suit is a torture chamber.

Mary Ann clutches his right arm. Robbie is off to the other side, somewhere, but he doesn't look at Michael, and Michael thinks he should offer the same courtesy.

The minister recites a litany of words as the walnut box descends.

He doesn't hear them. He doesn't try.

Mary Ann sways suddenly, as if she'll melt, fall away.

Michael wraps an arm behind her. He looks around for something. Something she could sit on. Something to shield her from the sun. There's nothing. No relief.

"Lean on me," he whispers, and she does.

He splays his feet apart, braces tightly to hold her weight.

Beads of sweat break out on his face and neck, a dizziness sets in. It's too hot, too difficult, too much. Too many minutes that pass like weeks, too many minutes in a row.

His eyes find Robbie in the crowd, he tries to go away in his head. Tries to see him as a young boy, standing at the train station.

What did you think when I left, Robbie? You never said.

Robbie's eyes come up to meet his, as if Michael's been thinking too loudly. Michael smiles politely and looks away.

· ★ ·

After the funeral, Mary Ann has a dozen or so people over to the house. Michael knows none of them. Just Mary Ann and Robbie.

He makes it his job to stay close to Mary Ann and provide support.

People seem to wonder who he is and why he's forming almost her entire support system, but no one asks straight out, and Mary Ann doesn't volunteer the information.

Every time Michael looks over at Robbie, sitting on the end of the couch in the corner of the living room, he catches Robbie staring back. Finally he goes over to him and sits down.

"Hey," Michael says.

"Hey."

An awkward silence.

Then Michael says, "Sorry you had to take the store."

"Well, it wasn't your fault."

Michael assumes he means, This is not about you. You had no part in this.

But then Robbie says, "It's not like you came home from the war and then went off to California to make cartoons. That I might have resented. You can't resent a guy for dying."

"Sure you can. It's done all the time."

"Not by me. I didn't resent that. The only thing I couldn't get past—" Then he stops himself. "No, never mind. It doesn't even matter."

"Go ahead," Michael says. "Spill it. You might feel better."

Robbie sighs. "I don't know if you ever thought about the chronology of this, but I hit the war pretty late in the game. It was 1945 before I was old enough to get myself drafted. So I was only there a couple of months. Not enough time for my number to come up. Oh, I mean, I know it's not that easy. Guys were there for years without a scratch and guys got killed their first day. It just seems like the odds are against you, the longer you stay. Anyway, it's not my fault I was younger and missed most of the war. But then I get home . . . I get home and Mom has this look in her eyes . . . I mean, she hugged me and said welcome home and thank God you're okay and all that, but there was this thing in her eyes, like . . ."

Robbie seems stalled, unable to finish, so Michael finishes for him.

"Like, why you and not Walter?"

"So you don't deny she loved you more."

"Couldn't very well deny that, no."

They sit in silence for a moment. Michael is wondering if he should apologize, and if so, how. But it's hard to apologize for what someone else did.

He looks over at Robbie, sees that he's breaking. Not in a bad way. You have to tear something down to rebuild it. Motorcycle, building, person.

He says, "You know, Robbie. When you went overseas in '45 . . . I was there with you."

Robbie pulls in a great, sharp breath. He opens his mouth to speak, then stops. Michael sees his mouth quiver. Realizes he is going to cry.

"I knew that," Robbie says. But it's so distorted, he has to breathe deeply and try again. The tears have let go now, as if Michael had accidentally torn a great hole in Robbie and let them out all at once. "I knew that. It was a secret I had with myself. One of those secrets about the world that just stays with you. Nobody else ever has to know. I've been thinking about it in the last few days. Thinking if Walter could do that, maybe he could do this."

"Is that why you came all the way out here?"

"Part of it. I probably would have anyway, for Mary Ann. I love Mary Ann." Robbie mops at his face with his handkerchief. "Damn. I hate crying in public. Hate it."

Michael throws an arm around his shoulders.

"Well, look at it this way, Robbie. You are at a funeral."

Robbie looks around, as if to satisfy himself that his behavior is right in place. "Good point, thanks. I'm sorry I was so crappy to you before."

"Oh, that's okay. You were pretty much always crappy to me."

One quick beat, and then they both let out a good snort of laughter. Now they are out of place at a funeral, and people turn to look.

"I'm sorry," Michael says. "You know how I meant that, right?"

"Yeah, I do. It's okay. We weren't very good at showing emotion in our family."

"Maybe we can still get better at it."

"How? How can our family get better at anything? Who's left?"

"We are," Michael says.

Robbie nods. Looks around the room. Blows his nose. Then he looks back at Michael and nods three more times, looking surer this time.

· ★ ·

When the last of the guests have gone, Michael putters around with Mary Ann, helping her clean up. They don't talk about what they've lost. They just exist together, two people who have lost.

They just clean up.

At bedtime, Mary Ann says, "I hate to make you sleep on that couch. It's so uncomfortable. It's such a big bed. You know how I mean that, right?"

"I do," he says. "I think we have our heads straight on that now."

He sleeps beside her in a pair of Andrew's pajamas, as if they do this every night.

In a dream, he finds himself sitting with Andrew at his hospital bed.

Andrew smiles at him, which he never once did in real life. Not this life, anyway. "I want you to take care of her," he says.

Michael shakes his head firmly.

"She's a strong woman, Andrew. She doesn't need anybody to take care of her. She's stronger than both of us put together."

Andrew nods. "You're right. That's the biggest mistake I made with her."

"She'll forgive you."

Then he falls into nonsense dreams, dreams that mean nothing, that are only what they are. Dreams.

CHAPTER FORTY-NINE

Mary Ann

She calls a realtor friend in Ocean City who rents her an apartment, sight unseen. It's near the ocean, and whatever it looks like, it will do for the interim. It may not be where she lives indefinitely, but for a time it will be home.

Michael stays over to help her pack.

It's a five-day process.

Some of the years of clutter will have to go into storage, or be sold or given away. Most of it is just that—clutter. Things Andrew couldn't bring himself to part with. If it were up to her, their lives never would have contained all this clutter. She prefers to let things go their way.

Michael amasses a van load. Things he wants to take home with him. Tools from the garage, lawn chairs, a few of Andrew's old suits that never looked so good on Andrew. A photo of Walter and Andrew in Atlantic City.

A picture of Mary Ann at the senior prom.

It's something she hasn't seen for years, that photo. They just stumble upon it one day. It's really only half the photo. Just her, with Walter cut away. It's dog eared, and pockmarked.

When they find it, Mary Ann says, "This looks like it's been through the war."

Michael says, "It has."

He tells her it was in Walter's pocket when he died. She wants to know why Walter cut himself out of it, but Michael never really says. He just says, You know Walter. You know how he was.

Then they uncover some newer treasures. A picture of a crazy kid and an old fool on a half-finished porch, mud and grease on their faded clothes.

He argues when she gives it to him, but she assures him she's kept the negative in a safe place.

In the end he accepts everything she offers.

But with all her belongings in cartons, packed onto a moving van and hauled away, the item she's been searching for never surfaces.

She never finds Walter's Purple Heart.

For almost five days it is carefully not mentioned. On the last day he breaks down and asks about it.

He says, "If you could bring yourself to part with it, it would mean a lot to me. For the first time in forty years, I'm not afraid of it. I wouldn't get sick to my stomach looking at it."

She has to admit to him that it's gone. It seems like an odd thing to lose, and there's nowhere besides the house it could be. It's a mystery, but one they can't stay here forever to solve. She promises that if she finds it during the unpacking, she'll send it right along.

He sits staring at the prom photo, a good bit after they both know it's time to go.

"Let me give you a piece of advice about that," she says. "Put that away in a drawer and only look at it on special occasions. If you don't, it'll lose all its meaning. You won't see it after a while."

He smiles and tucks the photo into his shirt pocket. She walks him to his van.

"Are you leaving right now?" he asks.

"As soon as you drive away."

He nods, as if that requires great thought. He doesn't move.

He says, "Do you forgive him?"

"Which him?"

"Andrew."

"Give me time."

"Okay. You've got time. You've got until next April 17th. That's when I'm first coming out to visit you."

"Is that a coincidence, or did you know that's Walter's birthday?"

"I knew. I thought we'd get some flowers. Take them to the cemetery. Tell him what's happened in the past year. That we love him. That sort of thing. It's a tradition."

He slides an arm around her waist and pulls her close. They wrap in each other's arms like it's a permanent arrangement.

She says, "You look more like him now than you ever did. Now he's like a foundation for you to build a house on."

"You're a good woman, Mary Ann."

"I am, aren't I?"

She pulls away, laughs.

He says, "You sure you don't want me to stay?"

"Of course I want you to stay. Now go away. You have a house to build."

"Yeah. Well. The foundation's strong. So I've got a good start."

He climbs into his van and heads for home.

CHAPTER FIFTY

Michael

He steps out of the van to the greeting of cool air, creek sounds, the sound of his heels on the wooden boards of the bridge.

The house looks the same. Like half a house. But not for long.

Dennis comes out on the porch to meet him.

"Man, I thought you died, or moved away, or something."

He smiles but doesn't answer. He did die, he did move away, but he's here now. Home.

Dennis says, "Things have changed around here, man."

Michael looks around. Everything looks the same.

"Is that a joke?"

"No, really. Major progress."

He runs inside and emerges with a cordless telephone.

"You telling me we got a phone line and everything?"

"At my own personal expense."

"I am impressed, Dennis."

He clicks the phone to talk, listens to the dial tone. Music. Rivals the wind in the trees.

"You got lots of mail, Mike. It's all on the kitchen table."

In the kitchen, he takes down a paper grocery bag, weeds the junk mail into it.

Three bills remain, plus a good catalog, a letter from Robbie, and a small, flat package postmarked Albuquerque, New Mexico.

He opens the letter from Robbie first.

Dear Michael,

I've thought a lot about our conversation. I'd like to write, talk on the phone, anything. I'd like to come out to visit, if that would be okay. I keep wishing Mom had gotten a chance to see you. I mean, while she was alive. She would have believed, I think. She'd know her own son.

After you left, I wondered if anyone had told you about Katie. If not, I'll wait until we're sitting down together sometime.

I also wondered if there were things you would want to ask.

Please feel free to call or write anytime.
Love,
   Robbie

He folds it carefully, places it back in its envelope.
Then he opens the package. And it's not from Mary Ann.
It's from Andrew. Inside is a small, flat case. Familiar looking.
An enclosed cardboard sheath contains the photo of the four
musketeers, and a note.

At first he thinks he's dreaming, or witnessing magic. But
he checks the date on the letter and sees it was written the day
before Andrew's heart attack. He looks again at the post-
mark. It probably arrived the day after he left home.

He opens the case, touches the medal, its purple ribbon,
takes it out and pins it to his shirt.

He reads the note.

Steeb,
   This photo really belongs to you, because it was
your five bucks that bribed the photographer to take
it. I was just holding it for you.
   Enclosing one other item I thought you might
want.
   Sincerely,
      Andrew

He sits out on the second-floor balcony and warms up on
his saxophone. It's been too long. He's rusty, but it comes
back to him.

He knows he needs to take a little time out to play now, before it's time to get to work.

Dennis comes out to the porch underneath him, walks out onto the grass.

Michael stops playing.

Dennis says, "I don't know what all you just been through, man, but I see they gave you a medal for it."

"I deserve it."

"From the look of you, I'd say you do."

"I'm going to finish this house, Dennis."

"Using what for money?"

"Using money for money. I'm going to work for it."

"Work? Man, did you say work? Who are you and what have you done with Michael?"

"I'm serious, Dennis. If I can build this house, I can build somebody else's house for money. Work by day, put this place together nights and weekends."

Dennis laughs, shakes his head, kicks divots of dirt and grass from under the toes of his boots.

"When will you have time to get high, man?"

"I won't."

"If I see it, I'll help with it. But first I have to see it."

He disappears into the house again.

Michael picks up his saxophone and nurses music out of it, bends and pushes the notes until the evening turns to dusk.

Then he goes inside after the phone, brings it out onto the balcony with him.

He gets the number from long distance information, then dials Robbie at home.

A woman answers.

"Is Robb there, please?"

He almost asks for Robbie, then corrects himself.

He hears the sound of young boys yelping and playing in the background.

"Hello?"

"Robbie."

"Michael?"

"Yeah, it's me. I just got your letter. Are those your kids in the background?"

"Those are my grandkids."

"Oh. Oh, yeah."

"I'm glad you called, Michael."

"Well, I was going to write, but I wanted you to know something. As soon as possible. I wanted you to know that Mary Ann took me to see Mom a few days before she died. And you were right. She knew."

A long silence. Then Robbie says, "I'm glad."

In the ensuing silence, Michael closes his eyes. He listens to the creek, the wind in the leaves, the sounds of home. He opens his eyes to see that the moon is up. He looks to the bridge, as if he'll see the ghost of Mary Ann, dangling her feet over the water. But he knows the time of ghosts is over.

He also knows this isn't why he called.

He says, "Mary Ann told me about Katie."

"Oh. You know, I'm kind of glad. I didn't want to have to be the one."

"Answer me something, Robbie. Did you ever want to kill that guy she was married to?"

A pause, then, "I almost did once. Went over while she was out of town to have a talk with him. He was just a little guy. I picked him up by the collar and told him if he laid a hand on my sister again, I'd kill him. Seems like he eased up on her then. But she didn't ease up on herself. Know what I mean?"

"Yeah, I think I do. Look, Robbie. I'm beating around the bush here. I called to ask you something, but it's so incredibly stupid . . ."

"No, go ahead, Michael. I won't think it's stupid."

"Oh, but you'd have to. I mean, of all the things for me to want to know . . . Anyway, here goes. Do you remember old Mrs. MacGurdy from down the street?"

"It'd be kind of hard to forget her. What an awful woman. Crazy, too."

"What was the name of that cat? That real old cat?"

He waits for his answer. It's been too long. Robbie won't remember.

"Oh, gosh, Michael."

"It was either Angel or Henrietta."

"Well, it definitely wasn't Henrietta, because Henrietta was an Airedale."

"Really? Andrew thought it was Henrietta."

"No, he was confused. That was an Airedale she had later. After the cat died. After the war. It must have been Angel. Andrew just got confused."

"That's what I tried to tell him."

"Too late to say I told you so, huh?"

"I guess."

"Hey, Michael. . . ."

He waits, hears the strain, the discomfort. Robbie wants to say something. Michael wants to help.

"Yeah, what is it, Robbie?"

"I think I just wanted to say that I really loved my brother, Walter."

"Yeah. In case you didn't know, he loved you, too. Even if he wasn't always very good at showing it. As soon as I get my house done, I'm going to have you come visit."

"I'll look forward to that."

They say good-bye, Michael clicks off the phone. Stares at it in admiration. A real phone. Progress.

A new van. That's next.

The sky is still light, but night settles in. The first stars appear.

Michael stands at the edge of the balcony, cups his hands around his mouth, and shouts up into the night.

"I told you so, Andrew!" He smiles to no one, then says, more quietly, "And if you don't believe me and Robbie, ask Mrs. MacGurdy."

Dennis comes out again, stares up at him, and tells him he's being weird.

Not anymore, he thinks. The time of weird is over.

He wants to call Mary Ann, but he won't. Not for a few weeks at least. Not until she can settle in. In her new apartment, in her head, her heart.

She'll try to achieve some kind of balance. He doesn't want to joggle her elbow. He'll wait.

He jumps down off the balcony, hands Dennis his phone back, sleeps straight through the night in his own room.

At home.

With himself.